COWBOY DOWN

KINGS OF MONTANA, BOOK 1

VANESSA GRAY BARTAL

DRY CREEK PRESS

PROLOGUE

*L*ayla Smith tapped her foot impatiently, waiting for the elevator to arrive. Showing up ten minutes early for her appointment was one way of trying to ease her anxiety. This was the day she had dreaded since she learned of its existence a year ago. Yesterday was her eighteenth birthday, but she felt no elation over the event, only dread. She was free, but her freedom came with a price tag. No longer was she a ward of the state; now she was fully on her own.

For years she had hated the tethers that bound her to the welfare system, hated any hint of her foster child status. But now that those tethers were about to be severed, she found herself nervous about what came next. Since she was fourteen, the state had provided her food, clothing, housing, and education. Now that she was on her own she would be handed three hundred dollars and a hearty farewell. She had nowhere to go; no job, no house, no prospects, and no family.

The elevator finally arrived. With trembling fingers, she pushed the button for Mr. Mather's floor. He was the last person she would meet with in the system. After this, she was officially on her own. Her emotions were mixed; she was anxious to get it over with, and yet her fear of the unknown made her dread the upcoming meeting.

The building was deserted, furthering her anxiety. Throughout the years, rumors had swirled about Mr. Mather; rumors stating that he offered additional assistance if foster kids were willing to perform certain favors. No one ever said exactly what those favors entailed, but after so many years in the system, Layla didn't need to use much imagination to figure out what they might be. Her lips pressed tightly together. No matter how frightened she was about her future, there was no way she would degrade herself for continued security. *Maybe the rumors aren't true,* she told herself. But doubts nagged in the back of her mind. She had tried to get an appointment first thing in the morning. Mr. Mather had insisted he had no available appointments during business hours, but he would be willing to meet with her at the end of the day. Desperation to get it over with compelled her to agree, but now she was regretting her decision.

If only she had a cell phone, she would have it ready to dial for help. Unlike some of her fellow foster kids, she hadn't lost faith in the justice system. Maybe it was because she hadn't been forcibly removed from her home, or maybe because she simply refused to become cynical. Whatever the reason, she felt the police were on her side and would do their best to help her, should she need them.

As she stepped into the hallway, she scanned the horizon hoping for a payphone, but there was none in sight. Would anyone hear her if she screamed? There was a fast food restaurant on the corner. Could she make it there for help if something happened? She paused again with her hand on the door to the office. What *exactly* had she heard about Mr. Mather? Had he ever attacked anyone? Had anyone ever refused him and been able to leave unscathed?

She bit her lip, her hand quaking slightly on the knob. How important was the money? Could she turn around and walk away without it? Her head swiveled to look at the elevator as she mentally reviewed her assets. One suitcase, a few clothes, a pair of shoes, and a toothbrush wouldn't get her far. Three hundred dollars might mean the difference between food and starvation, life and death. She would have to get the check. She would simply hope for the best-- that Mr.

Mather would immediately sense she wasn't the type of girl who would say yes to whatever he asked.

With that thought in mind, she steeled her spine and opened the door. As she expected, the secretary was gone. There were three inner doors, and Mr. Mather's name was clearly labeled on one of them. She took a step and stopped, wary all over again. Chill bumps rose on her arm. She tilted her head to the side, studying the door. There was a noise, and not a normal noise like the ticking of a clock or the slap of shoes on the floor. She had no idea what it was, but she suddenly didn't want to find out.

She took a step back until the door handle bumped her spine. The rational portion of her brain told her to step forward toward the office again. There was nothing to fear. Her undo anxiety was a symptom of her desire to get the meeting over with. But something, intuition maybe, told her to run.

Before she could decide what to do, the inner door to Mr. Mather's office opened. Time seemed to freeze, but everything took place in an instant. A man stepped out of the office, a gun in his hand. Behind him Mr. Mather lay sprawled in his chair, a gaping hole in his head. For a split second, her eyes met those of the murderer. They froze, staring, sizing each other up, and then he took a step.

Run!

The thought slammed into her brain a split second before it compelled her feet to action, but he was already upon her. She sprinted, not waiting for the elevator, and practically fell down the stairs in her haste. At first, her mind was too muddled with panic to scream or form any coherent thought. She only knew that she had to get away or he would kill her, and she also understood the likelihood that she *wouldn't* get away. He was a trim, athletic-looking guy; she was a panicked girl wearing ballet flats. But then, miraculously, he tripped on the top step. Cursing, he slid a few steps, grasping the railway to stop his descent. Her peripheral vision saw his fall, but she didn't turn back. If anything, she put more speed into her sprint. This was her only chance.

When she burst through the doors of the building, she tried

screaming, but there was no one around. Praying incoherently that it would still be open, she ran to the fast food restaurant and sobbed in relief when she saw it was crowded. Wasting no time with decorum or etiquette, she ran behind the counter and crouched to the floor.

A group of concerned/angry employees crowded around her and began to ask questions. Somewhere along the way she had begun to hyperventilate. The words would barely form behind her numb lips, but she kept repeating the same phrase until at last someone did what she told them to do.

"Call the police," she murmured, over and over, her voice rising in volume until at last she was shouting.

After that, everything was a blur. The police arrived and took her into their custody. She felt his eyes on her as she sat in the back of the cruiser. He could be watching from anywhere, waiting for an opportunity to kill her.

"Is this car bullet proof?" she asked.

For some reason the officer laughed as if she had told a funny joke. "Yes, honey. You don't have anything to worry about. No street thug is going to waste his time on you." He turned on the radio and began singing a country tune.

Frowning, she hunched farther down into the seat. Her confidence in law enforcement was waning. Somehow she understood that the murderer was no ordinary street thug. He was dressed in expensive clothes, and he looked calm and well-groomed. But soon her faith in the justice system would be restored. Several hours later, she was handed over to a federal marshal and placed in protective custody. The marshal, a handsome, brawny man, appeared fully capable of protecting her. As if to ease her fears even further, he talked her through every step of the process, tolerantly answering her questions without talking down to her.

"A partial print was found at the scene," he said. "We've matched it to four other known murders, and the man never leaves a witness alive. We're taking you into protective custody until we can attempt to locate him."

The marshal talked her through the details of what would happen while she was in custody, patiently answering her questions as they arose. Finally there was one question left to be answered.

"Where are you taking me?" she asked, her hands twisting nervously in her lap.

He smiled. It was the smile of someone who had an inside joke and, although she didn't understand why, she found herself almost smiling along. "Somewhere where they'll never find you," the marshal said. "The safest place on earth; I'm taking you to Montana."

CHAPTER 1

Cade King stared sullenly at the desolate landscape. At least, it was desolate to him. Everyone else would probably see the first signs of a lavish spring; the thick green grass, bluebirds, and tulips. But Cade's world had been black and white for the last six months, and to him everything looked dry and dead.

"Today's the day."

His older brother, Coy, waltzed into the room and plopped on the chair across from him. Coy was the only person he knew who could be described as waltzing when he walked. He was a happy-go-lucky, cheerful person who always walked with a light quickstep.

"Did you hear me?" Coy asked. "I said today."

"I heard," Cade said.

"A girl is coming to live here," Coy continued, undaunted by Cade's lack of enthusiasm. "A *girl*. And she's your age. The last girl who lived here was Mom." He shuddered at the mental comparison between their mother and the new, unknown girl.

"Mmm, hmm," Cade said, not removing his gaze from the window.

"She might be pretty," Coy added.

Cade winced. He hoped not. It was bad enough a girl was going to be living with them. If she were ugly, he might have a chance at being friends with her, but if she was pretty he would avoid her like the plague she was. He'd had enough of pretty girls in his lifetime.

Coy blew out an exasperated breath. "C'mon, man. You used to be fun. Now you're as stuffy as Cam and Josh. Cheer up. Snap out of it."

If he had the energy, he would have rolled his eyes. For Coy, who had never been depressed a day in his life, snapping out of a bad mood was as easy as changing his underwear. For Cade, it was less simple. His lack of response further irritated his brother until at last he stormed from the room. Cade resumed his lackluster inspection of the yard.

Time phased in and out until at last a pickup truck pulled into the yard. Previously Cade had wondered if he would feel some sense of elation or wonder over the newcomer. Coy hadn't been this excited since the Christmas he received his white Stetson hat as a present, and even their usually taciturn brothers Cameron and Josh were aflutter with nerves. But Cade felt nothing. His emotions, like his position at the window, remained unchanged.

He heard his cousin's voice and knew he should go say hello, but he had no energy to observe proper manners. His mother would be ashamed, but she wasn't here, so he stayed at the window. He hoped they wouldn't come to him, but of course they did. The soft, lilting voice of the girl drew nearer until curiosity finally broke through his malaise and compelled him to turn and look at her.

Please let her be ugly. He sent up one last, desperate prayer then turned to look. Unconsciously, he sucked in a breath. She wasn't ugly. She was beautiful. It wasn't that she was pretty, although she was. Her hair was shoulder-length and dark, almost black. Her eyes were the same color, and they were rimmed by long lashes. Her beauty was subtle and not the kind to win pageants, but that wasn't what Cade found so alluring. He was drawn in and captivated by her expression. Her chin was set in a determined, defensive expression, as if she were preparing to defend herself from a blow. He might have thought she was hard-edged, except for the soft, vulnerable light in her limpid eyes. Everything about her seemed to scream "protect me," and it was that thought that caused the knife to twist in Cade's chest. He couldn't protect her; he couldn't protect anyone.

* * *

LAYLA WAS BEWILDERED and overwhelmed by her new surroundings. She had never set foot outside the city, and now she was literally in the middle of nowhere. No wonder Marshal Wright had said no one would be able to find her on his cousins' ranch. She doubted it was even on a map.

First they had flown for hours and when she thought they couldn't get any more remote, they drove for three hours after leaving the airport. She had yet to see a cow or horse, but she had seen land, lots and lots of land.

"Where is this place?" she had asked when they landed.

"Montana," Marshal Wright had answered.

"Where in Montana?" She wasn't a geography wizard, but she knew enough to realize Montana was huge.

"The less you know about your location, the better off you'll be," the marshal had said. On the long drive, he explained his family connection to the ranch.

"My aunt and uncle own the ranch. My uncle has rheumatoid arthritis pretty bad. The cold weather bothered him, so he and my aunt bought a condo in Arizona and live there full time. He turned over the care of the ranch to his four sons, my cousins."

She had nodded, taking in everything he said as if she understood, but when they arrived on the ranch she stared in surprise. First of all, the ranch was much larger than anything she had ever imagined. Once she had lived in a foster home that had an acre of land, and she had thought it was sprawling. Now that acre looked like a centimeter on a ruler in comparison to this vast spread. Second, the cousins were much younger than she guessed.

The oldest two were twins, though when Marshal Wright introduced them she did a double take. They didn't look or act anything alike. Obviously they were fraternal, and the fact that they were such polar opposites was amusing to her.

"This is my cousin, Cameron," Marshal Wright said, indicating a tall, unsmiling man who held out his hand to her.

"You're very welcome here," he said. Even though his tone was reserved and solemn, she knew he meant it. Her heart warmed and tears swam in her eyes, clouding her vision. He stared at her, horrified. "Uh, I have to check something in the north pasture." He mounted a nearby horse and took off at what she assumed was a gallop.

The next cousin in line chuckled as he watched his brother's retreating backside. "I'm Coy." After introducing himself, he grabbed her hand and pumped it enthusiastically. His face-cracking smile was contagious. Her answering smile cleared away the vestiges of her tears. "We're so happy to have you here," he said. "Really, you have no idea." He smiled again.

He was handsome, as Cameron had been, but she was too nervous to feel any flutter of attraction to him.

"Thank you," she said shyly. She bit her lip and turned to the next brother in line, waiting to be introduced.

"This is Josh," Marshal Wright said. "He's the baby of the bunch at sixteen."

Josh whipped off his white cowboy hat and wrung it miserably between his hands. His cheeks were so pink they were crimson, and he wouldn't quite meet her eyes.

He's shy, she thought, her heart immediately warming to him. So far he was the handsomest brother, although his looks were just beginning to shed their last signs of babyhood.

"Pleased to meet you, Josh," she said pleasantly.

He nodded briefly before jamming his hat back on his head. She turned to study the house to give him a reprieve from further conversation. By her calculations there was one brother missing.

"How's Cade?" Marshal Wright asked.

Coy let out an exaggerated sigh. "The same. You should say hello. Maybe the sight of you will cheer him up." Despite his words, his voice held no hope that anything would work to cheer the other boy up. She wondered what was wrong with him that made him so despondent, but it didn't take her long to find out.

After a quick tour of the house, they approached a closed door.

"This is the den," Coy announced. He had called out labels for every room they visited. He possessed an enthusiastic, boyish charm she found endearing. He threw open the door and stepped inside, indicating the interior of the room with a flourish of his hand. At first she was distracted by the cozy interior; it was manly, but not oppressively so. It was as if a woman had designed the room with a man in mind, but kept a few feminine touches for herself. There was a wall full of bookshelves on the far side. A wooden, leather top desk was pressed beneath one window, and there was a fireplace with two cozy-looking chairs. Of all the rooms she had been shown, this one was her favorite. Immediately she wanted to grab a book and curl up beside the fire.

"And this is our brother, Cade." Coy's bright tone hadn't changed, but there was still something in it that alerted her senses. She turned, ready to face she knew not what, but nothing could have prepared her for what she found.

A boy sat several feet away, his lip stuck out in an almost pouty expression. At first her eyes were riveted on his mouth as she realized he wasn't pouting on purpose, his lips were just naturally that full. Then, slowly, her eyes traveled up his face to meet his eyes. She blinked in astonishment as she took in his expression. *Wounded* was the best word for it. Something had happened to him that had hurt him, perhaps irreparably. They stared at each other without blinking for what felt like a very long time until at last Coy cleared his throat.

"Cade, this is our new houseguest, Layla. Layla, our brother, Cade. You two are the same age."

Reluctantly, it seemed, Cade held out his hand to her, and she realized why he hadn't stood up. It was because he couldn't. He dropped his hand, rolled his wheelchair forward until he was sitting right in front of her, and then he spoke.

"Are you too good to shake the hand of a cripple?"

CHAPTER 2

At first Layla was too stunned to be embarrassed. Was he joking with her by pretending to be angry? After all, who was that abrasive to a stranger? Then she realized he thought she was staring at him in mute surprise because he was in a wheelchair. How could she possibly explain she was staring at him because she thought him handsome, and because her lightning bolt attraction to him had caught her off guard?

"I," she began, but then a rescue came from a surprising source.

"If you can't talk like a gentleman, then don't talk at all," Josh said. "What would Mom say if she heard you speak like that?"

To her further chagrin, Cade flushed in embarrassment and rolled away from her.

"Sorry," he muttered.

"No, it's my fault," she assured him, trying desperately to think up an explanation for her silence. "I'm afraid I'm a little overwhelmed by everything. I'm usually not so…whatever I am right now." She smoothed her hand nervously over her hair.

Coy slapped her reassuringly on the back, so hard she stumbled forward a step. He dropped his hand and looked sheepish. "Sorry.

None of us is used to having girls around here for any length of time. We're going to have to get used to you."

She smiled. "And I'll have to get used to you."

Marshal Wright nodded his head approvingly. "Good. Now that's settled, I'd better be on my way."

Her peaceful, secure feeling fled. She clasped her hands to her chest in a plaintive gesture. "You're leaving?" So far in her ordeal, he had been her rock and guiding light. With him, she felt safe and protected. Without him, she was alone in the middle of Montana with four cowboys for company.

Marshal Wright nodded. "I wish I could stay, but then how would we ever catch the bad guy?" He grinned at her, reminding her of Coy who was giving her the same look.

"Don't worry," Coy said. "Everyone in Montana is armed, and we can spot a stranger a mile away, especially a city-dweller. Anyone tries to come after you here, he'll find himself hogtied quicker than you can open your mouth to call for help." Because she looked unconvinced, he continued. "All of us sleep with loaded guns under our pillows. In fact, you'd better not go creeping through the halls at night, or…"

She blanched, causing Josh to knock Coy roughly on the back of the head. Coy winced and rubbed his head.

"I was just kidding about that last part. We do sleep with loaded guns, but we would never make the mistake of…"

Josh raised his hand again and Coy broke off again. "Never mind. The point is, we'll take good care of you, and you're safe here."

She smiled and patted his shoulder reassuringly. "Thank you. You'll never know how much I appreciate this." Throughout the entire exchange, she had felt Cade's eyes on her, but when she looked at him, he looked away and pretended to stare through the window. So far he was the one blip on her radar. The other brothers had made clear her welcome, but she knew Cade wished her gone. For some reason, that thought hurt more than it should. She wasn't usually so sensitive, but right now she wanted nothing more than to go to him and plead her case because, suddenly, she really wanted to stay.

It was worse than Cade thought. Not only was she pretty, but she was *nice*. At first he had hoped she was one of those shallow pretty girls who were so into themselves they didn't notice when someone rebuffed them. But then he had tried to be rude to her on purpose and fell flat on his face, so to speak. His conscience still smote him. He knew even before Josh spoke that he had done something wrong, but to be called out in public by his too-serious little brother was mortifying. On top of the humiliation of having the girl see him confined to his cursed chair, the embarrassment was almost more than he could stand. He wanted her to leave and never come back, the sooner the better.

But of course he was the only one who felt that way. Josh, Coy and even Cam were already half in love with her. Of course, they were so starved for female companionship she probably would have had the same effect if she had a humpback and two black teeth. The fact that she was pretty and charming was almost sensory overload.

He remained quiet while conversation swirled around him at supper that night. Listlessly, he pushed his food around his plate. Remembering the days when he worked and ate like a lumberjack caused his appetite to dim even further. Why should he be hungry? He did nothing to burn calories except sit and stare out a window all day.

He felt her eyes on him several times through the meal, increasing his anger. He refused to meet her gaze, not wanting to see the pity that would most likely be there. Instead he dropped his fork and rolled away from the table without a word to anyone. Let his brothers make excuses for him since they were so willing to chat up the newcomer.

THE APOLOGIES BEGAN IMMEDIATELY.

"He hasn't been himself since the accident. He's not normally like this, really. I'm sorry, things have been rough around here the last few months."

She nodded and smiled and tried to assure them her feelings weren't hurt, although they were. Maybe what they said was true;

maybe he had been surly for the last few months. But tonight it had been directed at her, and she couldn't help but take his rejection personally. Forcing a bright smile, she tried to push it from her mind.

The next day she rose early, almost as soon as the sun was up. But by the time she showered, dressed, and left her room, the King brothers were already outside. Well, three of them, anyway. She assumed Cade was still in the house, although she hadn't seen him. Didn't he eat? Last night he had barely picked at his food. No matter what, he was still a man. How did he survive on so little?

After a quick breakfast of toast and juice, she tidied the kitchen and turned to face the room, her hip resting on the counter. What should she do? She had never had so much uncluttered free time, at least not when she felt safe enough to enjoy it. During her summer hiatuses from school, she had spent her days anywhere but at the place where she lived. Most of the time, she went to the library and read, or went to the Laundromat and watched cable. Sadly, either of those places felt more comfortable to her than whatever house she was assigned to at the time.

But now she was in a sprawling and beautiful ranch home where she felt safe and cocooned from the world. And she was bored. What was wrong with her? Was she simply one of those people who was never happy? Her hand ran over the counter absently. What she wanted was a purpose. Rest and relaxation were nice, but they had a limit, and she had reached it yesterday.

Besides, hadn't Benjamin Franklin been correct when he said that guests, like fish, begin to smell after three days? The brothers seemed enthusiastic and welcoming, but she wasn't naïve enough to think those feelings wouldn't fade after the newness wore off. Eventually they would get tired of having a stranger in their midst, especially a stranger who didn't pull her weight. But she was reluctant to start any projects without the brothers' express permission.

One more day. She would spend the remainder of this day relaxing, and then tomorrow she would start contributing something. She had no idea what, since she didn't exactly know how to do anything on a ranch, but she would figure it out. With that in mind, she smiled and stretched, prepared to enjoy her last day of vacation. Strange how a different perspective could change everything. This morning she had felt the day stretching before her cavernously. Now, knowing it was her last chance to do nothing, she felt elated at the prospect.

She reheated another cup of coffee and sat at the kitchen table, thinking. There were two things she needed to decide this morning: What was she going to do to start helping out, and how was she going to enjoy her last blissful day of freedom? She smiled to herself, both at the prospect of work and relaxation.

CHAPTER 3

First things first, what was she going to do today? That one was a no-brainer. Whenever she had free time, she liked to fill it with books or television. Since she hadn't noticed a television on the ranch, she wasn't sure if they had one, let alone cable. But the den had been stuffed with books, and many of them looked brand new. The thought of the big, cozy chair by the fireplace called to her, along with the fluffy afghan that had been draped over the chair. It was June, and Chicago had been hot already, but Montana still felt brisk, like spring. Her two outfits were both short-sleeved and unsuited to the temperatures. As if to remind her of that fact, chill bumps rose on her arms and she tried to chafe them away.

"That's it," she announced to herself. The chill bumps were the incentive she needed to overcome her fear of invading Cade's personal space. She had barely glimpsed him yesterday, but she knew he was in the den. It seemed to be his preferred space. But surely there was room enough for her, wasn't there? He didn't own the room, she wouldn't make any noise, and she wouldn't bother him. Or at least that's what she told herself as she walked down the hall. In reality, her knees were quaking with uncertainty. Would he send her away? Should she simply take a book and go to her room to read?

Her nose wrinkled at that idea. She didn't want to lie in bed all day. That would be depressing. She wanted to stay in the den and enjoy the quiet beauty of the room. She had never been in a room with real wood paneling before. It was a sharp contrast to the fake plywood paneling in a couple of her foster homes.

Layla had always been one of those people who, despite her poverty, was drawn to the finer things in life. Before knowing the price tag on an item, she often gravitated toward the highest quality and therefore most expensive pieces. And then with a sigh she would realize the object was grossly out of her budget and move on to what she could afford. Still, she didn't covet the things that were out of her grasp. She simply appreciated them when she was near them. The lush richness of the materials in the den called to her, and she wanted to be in that room whenever possible.

The walk down the hallway was much too short, and then she was standing outside the den. To her relief, the door was open. Knocking would have felt degrading somehow. Cade's back was to her as he stared out the window. The pads of his fingers were pressed to the pane as he looked outside.

Layla crept into the room, took a book from the shelf, and picked up the afghan from the chair.

"I don't need that."

Cade's voice startled her and she whirled to look at him. He hadn't moved positions; was he talking about something outside the window?

"What?" she asked, uncertainty making her voice sound soft.

"If you were about to cover me with a blanket, I would rather you didn't." He turned to face her then and she wished he wouldn't have. His eyes burned with indignation and anger.

She knew she shouldn't, but she laughed a little bit before pulling herself back under control. He was like a little kid who wanted to do everything on his own with no help from mom. "Okay," she drawled. "Is it okay if I use it? I'm cold." She sat and covered herself with the blanket.

He had the good sense to look sheepish. Maybe he even blushed a little, she couldn't tell. "Oh. Sorry. I…my mom and girl cousins are always trying to cover me up, like now that I can't walk I'm suddenly freezing all the time. I guess I jumped to the wrong conclusion. Sorry."

She nodded, trying to keep her amusement contained. She had no idea why she found him funny right now, she just did. It wasn't like she was laughing at him; it was more like she wanted to share his amusement over his female relatives constantly trying to put blankets on him, although he didn't look amused. He looked annoyed. But he *should* be amused.

"Don't you think it's sort of funny?" she couldn't help asking.

Now it was his turn to look puzzled. "What?"

"That people keep trying to put blankets on you. I mean, I've never seen anyone who looks less like he needs a blanket tossed over him. The thought makes me laugh." She giggled and pressed the back of the book to her lips to try and stop.

He smiled at her as he envisioned himself grumpy and unwelcoming in his chair. What on earth had possessed people to try and cover him up? He might as well have been wearing a neon sign that flashed "Leave me alone." Why would anyone approach him with a blanket?

"Maybe they were trying to gentle me," he suggested. Whenever the horses were scared, they covered their eyes with blankets to try and calm them.

She smiled. "Or maybe they just love you," she said, returning to her book.

He stared at the book now covering her face. His anger was totally gone now, for the first time in a long time. Since the accident he had remained angry about anything and everything. And now it was gone, at least for a little while. He knew it would return, but this brief reprieve felt like a pause between two agonizing injuries. He could breathe easily without that nagging tightness in his chest. How did she do that? How did she diffuse his anger and make him see things from a different perspective? Of course his family loved him and hadn't meant to offend him with the blankets. How had he thought otherwise?

He shook his head to try and clear it, resuming his post at the window. She was dangerous to him. He knew it in the same way you knew a rattlesnake was dangerous, by the prickling of your skin and the acceleration of your heart. And, like the snake, her alarms were almost as loud. Her sweet laughter was enough to send him running in the other direction, figuratively speaking. Already he looked forward to hearing it, and that was terrible news for him. Not only was she temporary, but she was off limits to him. Why did he want to be near her when he should want to be as far from her as possible?

Despite his best attempts, he hadn't stopped thinking of her since they met. And now she was in this room, just a few feet away. And he didn't mind at all. In fact, he was glad she was here, a little too glad. He was almost giddy with the thought of her nearness. Already, he had sneaked a dozen peaks at her since her arrival. He stole another one now, letting his eyes linger.

She was uncommonly pretty with her dark hair, dark eyes, and pale complexion. Her cheek was pillowed on her hand and a gentle half-smile lingered on her lips. Was that smile because of their conversation, or was she amused by something in the book? What made her laugh or cry or scream with frustration?

His fist clenched and he fought a groan. What was wrong with him? Did he hate himself so much now that he had to punish himself by wanting what was so far out of his reach? Why couldn't he leave her alone and forget about her? Why couldn't she leave him alone or, even better, feel sorry for him? If she pitied him, he would hate her. But he sensed no pity in her, and that intrigued him even more. If she didn't pity him, then what did she feel?

The uncertainty and frustration caused his anger to flare to life once again. He welcomed it like an old friend. Anything was better than feeling like a lovesick loser, even if it was soul-twisting rage.

* * *

LAYLA FELL ASLEEP. She hadn't meant to, of course, but being curled up in the overstuffed chair with a warm blanket on top of her had made her drowsy. Her book was lying neatly on the coffee table in front of her and she didn't remember putting it there. Had Cade done it? Did it topple off the chair when she fell asleep, or did she place it there before falling asleep?

She stretched, looking around, but he wasn't in the room anymore. Down the hall in the kitchen, she heard the unmistakable sounds of supper being prepared. Not for the first time, she felt bad for the family. They had to work all day and then come home and make their supper at night. With that thought came inspiration. She bit her lip and bolted to the kitchen, startling the family as she skidded into view.

Almost immediately upon sight of her, Cade turned and wheeled himself down the hall to the den.

Coy shot her an apologetic smile, but she ignored it. She had bigger fish to fry right now.

"What can I do to earn my keep around here?" she asked.

They stared at her, momentarily stunned by her sudden outburst. Of course they didn't have the advantage of hearing the entire conversation and thought process in her head.

"You're our guest," Cam said at last. Layla had the sense that although he and Coy were twins, he functioned as the eldest brother, taking charge in all ranch matters.

"That's very sweet, but I'm supposed to be posing as your new housekeeper. Maybe I should actually become your housekeeper."

Coy and Cam chorused their disagreement again. Josh remained silent, but he looked troubled.

"I'm not good at sitting still," she told them. "Please, let me do something."

The brothers paused, looking at each other. Ever since their parents left they had taken turns doing the cooking, and their efforts were lackluster to say the least. Once a week someone came to do the cleaning and they somewhat kept up on their laundry, but they all knew when their mother came for a visit she would be appalled at the state of the house. Their desire for the type of domestic comfort a female could provide waged war with their chivalrous sense of hospitality.

"Do you know how to be a housekeeper?" Cameron asked.

She bit her bottom lip. "Well, no. I don't actually have any skills." *Except surviving a system where I'm a number,* she thought. "But I want to learn, and I've always been able to do whatever I set my mind to. If you'll be patient with my failures, I'll try really hard to do a good job."

Reluctantly, they agreed. What did they have to lose? They all believed that women were gifted by nature with the ability to cook and run a household because that was the example they'd received in their mother. They figured her failures couldn't be worse than their successes.

Layla was elated. The state had put her through high school and provided for her basic elements, but it hadn't taught her any real skills. She was unemployable. But now she had a chance to learn real skills without the pressure of being paid to do so. She would learn how to cook and clean, and maybe when this was all over she would be able to get a job as a housekeeper. Or maybe she could start her own cleaning service. Her mind ran wild with the thought of owning her own business.

From his den retreat down the hall, Cade heard Layla's happy chatter and almost smiled. Once upon a time he would have flirted with her to make her laugh and giggle as she was now. Probably he would have stolen an opportunity to kiss her, just to make sure she really liked him. But now he was a lonely outsider, sitting on the periphery and watching while everyone else talked and had fun. What bothered him wasn't that he was alone this night, but that his future stretched out before him in a lonely series of nights like these. His brothers would eventually grow up and fall in love. With the way things were going, maybe one of them would fall for Layla. In time, they would make lives for themselves with their wives and children. And he would remain alone because he was sure no one would ever love a sad, broken waste of a man like him.

CHAPTER 4

*L*ayla snuggled down into her covers, reluctant to leave her room. She had never had her own room before. For the last few years she had had at least one roommate, but usually the homes she was placed in were stuffed to capacity. Now she had an entire huge room to herself along with an attached bathroom. The feeling of being a princess tempted her into enjoying the comfort of bed awhile longer, but finally her desire to earn her keep won out.

She threw off the covers and made her bed. It was early, but necessity had made her an early riser. It was a good rule of thumb never to be the last one sleeping in a foster home and always the first one awake. Sleep was a vulnerability. She had seen more than one late riser attacked and beaten.

Although it was early, the house seemed deserted. A quick peek out the window showed the yard already bustling with activity. She wondered how early she would have to rise in order to be up before the brothers, and then wondered if she really wanted to. The sun was just starting to peek over the horizon; did they get up in the middle of the night?

She touched an empty coffee cup lying on the counter and found it still warm, telling her she had just missed them. That was a relief. She would only have to tweak her schedule a little if she planned to make breakfast for them.

The thought of cooking breakfast caused her to bite her lip in dismay. She turned in a slow circle, surveying the kitchen. What did they eat for breakfast, and how was she to cook it? And for that matter, what should she make for supper?

The cleaning portion of things didn't faze her. She had always kept her area neat because tidiness helped her fly under the radar. Maybe she had never formed any lasting bonds with any of her foster families, but they never had any complaints about the clean and quiet girl who always went to school and did what she was told.

But she had never even held a measuring cup in her hands. How did she know what to cook, or how to do it, or how much to make? What if she gave them all food poisoning? What if her food was raw or inedible? The task of learning which foods to prepare and how to prepare them seemed monumental.

She sank to a chair and looked around the large kitchen again. What she needed was a cookbook. There were none on the counters, so she stood and made a quick search of the cupboards. Nothing.

She sank to a chair again. She would have expected cookbooks to be kept in the kitchen, but what if they weren't? What if they were kept in the den with all the other books? Her stomach twisted with the thought of disrupting Cade in what was obviously his lair. But maybe he wasn't up yet. He had no reason to rise this early. Maybe he liked to sleep in a little bit. Crossing her fingers, she crept to the den and poked her head around the opening. The room was empty. She sighed in relief and took a tentative step inside.

A quick survey of the room revealed no cookbooks, but a laptop computer caught her eye. Tentatively, she took a step toward it and paused. She knew she could look up a million recipes on it, but Marshal Wright had warned her to stay off the internet. Realistically she understood that he wanted her to avoid signing in on a sight that might identify her and leave a digital footprint, but she was still wary. Never having owned a computer, she was barely literate on one. Although she knew it wasn't rational, she had the vague notion that the killer would be able to find her the moment her fingers touched the keys.

"Are you planning to pilfer our laptop?"

She whirled to find Cade sitting in the doorway. At first she recoiled from the implication that she was intending to steal, then to her amazement she realized he was teasing her. He was even almost smiling.

"I was thinking about it, but then I realized there probably aren't any pawn shops in Montana."

His smile increased. "Maybe in Helena, but that's hours away by car." He paused. "Did you need something?"

Was his question a subtle way of telling her to get out of his den, or did he truly want to help? She decided to take a leap and hope he was offering help. "A cookbook," she said. It sounded like a question.

"You're looking for a cookbook in the computer?"

She explained how she had been unable to find a cookbook and considered looking up recipes on the computer. "But your cousin told me to stay off the internet," she ended.

He nodded. "Do you want me to look something up for you?"

Her hands clasped under her chin. "Would you?"

He nodded and wheeled to the computer, keeping an eye on her the whole time. "Are you always this grateful when people do mundane things for you?"

She could have told him that no one had ever done anything for her, but she didn't. Instead she nodded and stood over him while he booted up the computer. He turned to look at her over his shoulder.

"You're hovering." He pointed to a chair and she sat.

"Sorry," she said.

He pressed the appropriate buttons until the internet was up. "What do you want me to look up?" he asked.

"Um…" She gave him a helpless look. "What do you and your brothers like to eat?"

"Beef," he answered.

She smiled. "I surmised that from the two freezers full of beef." She bit her lip and looked uncertainly at the computer, hoping it would miraculously tell her what to do. "I don't know how to cook beef. What do you eat with it? What's your favorite food?"

He was caught off guard by her hopeful, baleful look. "Lasagna," he said and cleared his throat.

Her face lit. "Lasagna. How hard can that be? Find a recipe for that, please."

He typed lasagna in the search engine and brought up almost a million hits.

"Um," she began, her doubts surfacing again. How could she choose among so many options? "I guess look for the highest-rated recipe."

He found one, printed it, and handed her the recipe. She folded it in half and shoved it to her side, deciding to look at it later when she could try to puzzle its meaning in private. "Thank you."

He nodded, still watching her like she was a zoo exhibit who at any moment might perform a mind-boggling trick.

"I guess I should get started cleaning," she said.

"Why are you cooking and cleaning?" he asked. "You're our guest."

"I like to earn my keep," she said. "And I want to learn how to do something, anything."

"Somehow I could have guessed you weren't one to sit on your laurels," he said.

She grinned. "I don't even know where my laurels are," she said. She stood and walked out the door, followed by the sound of his laughter.

Her smile dimmed as she reached the kitchen and pulled out the recipe. It was like reading a foreign language. She understood the list of ingredients, but had no idea where to find them or what to do with them. First things first, she realized the beef would need to thaw. She walked to one of the massive freezers and rooted around until she found what looked like ground beef.

The package wasn't labeled. The recipe called for a pound and a half. She bounced the package of beef in her hand, trying to determine if it felt like a pound and a half. Finally she remembered the scale in her bathroom. She took the beef to her room and laid it on the scale.

It was a perfect pound. She returned to the kitchen, set the beef on the counter and added another package to it to make two pounds. She started to leave and then turned to look at the beef again.

Was it okay to let beef thaw on the counter? And how long would it take? What if it wasn't thawed by the time she needed it? She sighed and pressed her fingers to her temple. Part of her was tempted to return to the den and ask Cade to look up how to thaw beef, but the thought of facing him with such a simple-minded request was too embarrassing. Instead she decided to leave the beef on the counter, hoping that it would be thawed in time for supper and also hoping she wouldn't give everyone salmonella or whatever it was people got from eating tainted beef.

She rooted around the closets and cupboards until she located cleaning supplies and decided on a plan of action. The house wasn't a pigsty; it was mostly picked up and clean. But her discerning eye located hidden dust, cobwebs, and grime that appeared to have been accumulating for some time. She scrubbed all the bathrooms from top to bottom, dusted and vacuumed, saving the den for last.

By the time she was ready to clean the den it was lunchtime. No one else appeared for lunch, so she assumed they either didn't eat or had packed lunches. She made a sandwich for herself and as an afterthought made one for Cade. He looked thin, too thin, and she guessed he didn't eat well. For some reason she tiptoed to the den, and then was glad she did. Cade sat slumped in his chair, asleep facing the window.

Gingerly, she set the sandwich and a glass of iced tea on the table beside him and crept from the room. The sight of him sleeping in his chair like an old man was sad. He was a young, virile guy. Why did he closet himself away in that room like a hermit? Was he lonely? Was he bored? He had to be. She wondered what happened to him and what he was like before.

She returned to the kitchen and stared at the recipe again. The first step said to brown the beef. What did that mean? Obviously she knew it meant to cook it, but for how long? How brown was brown?

"You look like you're studying for the SAT."

Cade's voice from the doorway startled her. She spun to see him framed in the doorway, his plate and glass on his lap. She rose to reach for them, but he bypassed her and set them on the sink himself.

"So what's up?" he asked.

She could have pointed out that he didn't know her well enough to assume she was upset, but since she actually was upset, she decided to unload her problems.

"I don't know how to cook. This recipe is confusing. The writer speaks in technical jargon as if she assumes I already know how to cook." She sank into the chair again. "I need one of those beginner books for kids that show how to boil water."

"Kid books don't show how to boil water because they're not allowed to use the stove," he pointed out.

"You know what I mean." She brightened. "Do you know how to cook?"

He shook his head. "We are the product of a mother who left us to men's work while she ran the kitchen like a workhorse. Food magically appeared at the end of the day with none of us knowing how it arrived. Now that we're on our own, I sort of regret never learning how to cook." He looked away with a frown.

She wanted to suggest learning together, but she was afraid he would reject her. Instead, she asked him to tell her where to find the ingredients she needed. "You'll save me a whole lot of time looking."

He gave her a rueful smile. "I have no idea where anything is kept in the kitchen. After our mom moved away, my brothers took over cooking." He shuddered. "I miss real food." That was only partially true. He'd had no appetite for months, but maybe he might if his brothers weren't such abysmal cooks. He tipped his head to study her. "You're worried about failing with the food."

She nodded. She looked miserable.

"Your food can't be worse than theirs," he assured her.

"I don't want it to be bad; I want it to be good."

"Oh, you're one of those," he said.

"One of what?"

"A perfectionist. No one is good when they first try something.

There's a learning curve for everything. Believe me when I tell you my brothers are so enthusiastic about your arrival, you could serve them platters of dirt and it would taste like manna to them."

She noticed he didn't include himself in that statement. "I suppose I'm going to have to jump in and do it," she said, standing.

He was tempted to hang around and watch her work, and the temptation surprised him. For so long he had only desired his own company. On the one hand, he was glad to know he could still respond to a pretty girl. On the other hand, the situation was hopeless and he had no intention of torturing himself by getting to know her better, no matter how intriguing he found her.

"I'll leave you to it," he said.

She watched him go with sad eyes. She was lonely, for the first time in a long time. Long ago she had learned to be content with her own company because she was never sure who she could trust. Other foster kids were either too messed up or too needy to befriend, and she didn't feel comfortable opening up to "normal" kids who might not understand her situation. So she remained alone and, for the most part, she didn't mind the solitude. But now she wanted someone to talk to, someone to banter with and ask questions of. She wanted Cade.

"But he doesn't want you," she whispered. With one last shake to clear her head, she turned toward the stove and began preparing supper.

CHAPTER 5

It was bad, but not inedible. The noodles were crunchy in some spots and soggy in others. The sauce was bland and the cheese was too salty. It fell apart when she served it, but everyone ate with relish.

Cade caught her eye over the table and, after observing his brothers' enthusiasm, gave her a secret smile. She returned his smile and tried to calm the frantic beating of her heart. Why she should have such a strange reaction to him out of all the brothers, she had no idea. Coy was openly interested in her and never let an opportunity pass to flirt with her. He was cute with light brown hair that curled slightly on the ends. His eyes were a greenish shade of brown, and he had a dimple in one cheek. She saw the dimple often because he was almost always smiling.

Cameron was nice looking, too. He didn't flirt with her, but he wasn't the flirting type. Still, she had the impression he would be interested in her if he weren't so busy running his ranch. His hair was a lighter shade of brown than Coy's. It might have curled if given the chance, but it was cropped close to his head, almost like a military crew cut. If he weren't a cowboy, he would make an excellent marine, she thought. He had that quiet, strong, disciplined nature the armed forces instilled. His eyes were a light shade of brown and he had no dimple. At least she didn't think he had a dimple. When he smiled, it was a controlled maneuver, as if he didn't want to let his face have too much fun. Like Coy, he was only twenty, but he seemed much older.

Josh had barely spoken two words to her since her arrival. Of all the brothers, he showed the least interest in her, although he was always unfailingly polite. He had even held her chair for her when she sat. She pictured him reading Emily Post at night in his bed and had to fight back a giggle. He was cute with hair the color of his saddle. Like Cameron, his hair was short, but not quite as severe. His eyes were a leafy shade of green, and he had two dimples. Despite the fact that he was only two years younger than her, there was something boyish and immature about him. Maybe it was the dimples in his slightly rounded cheeks. He might be one of those men who always looked like a kid, no matter how old he was.

And then there was Cade. Her heart turned over thinking his name. His hair was dark brown and long, hanging almost to his chin. He kept it tucked behind his ears and occasionally gave it an impatient push away from his face. His chin and cheeks were covered with a fine layer of stubble, but it did nothing to hide the perfection of his mouth. She had never seen lips so red or full. It was all she could do not to stare at them. But there were other things about his appearance that concerned her. His skin was an unhealthy pale color, as if he hadn't seen the sun in a long time. He was thin, but it was an unnatural thinness, as if he had recently lost a lot of weight after being robust. She studied his hair again and an idea occurred to her. Did he want to wear it long, or had he been unable to get out in order to have it cut?

Her mind jogged back to her first day here as she tried to remember what had been said about Cade. If memory served her correctly, he had been in his present state for months. What if his hair was driving him crazy, but he was unable to do anything about it? Conversation swirled around her as she tried to figure out how to ask him about it without offending him.

* * *

CADE SURREPTITIOUSLY WATCHED Layla throughout the meal. What did she think about when she stared at her plate that way? He choked down another bite of the lasagna as possibilities ran through his mind. Was she upset because her lasagna hadn't turned out perfectly? You would think it was the best food they had ever eaten if his brothers' reaction was any indicator. He should have explained to her that after a day working cattle she could set out sawdust and the brothers would inhale it.

With a pang of longing, he remembered the way it had felt to be that hungry. There was nothing like physical exertion to work an appetite into a frenzy. Maybe that was why he hadn't been hungry since the accident. His body knew he was doing nothing to deserve food. Briefly he reminisced about days spent in the saddle with his brothers. They had competed over everything; who could work the hardest, who could ride the fastest, who could eat the most, who could spit the farthest. And who could kiss the most girls. He smiled and slid his glance to Coy. That had been their private competition. Cameron had no interest in competing, and Josh was too shy. Despite the lack of available females, he and Coy never seemed to have any trouble finding one. Over the years he had perfected his lines until the girls he encountered became putty in his hands. At the last count, he had been up by two girls.

His smile fled. He focused on his plate again. He knew Coy hadn't surpassed his goal because he had been too busy at the ranch. His brothers had to pick up the slack his absence caused. He was a burden to them in more ways than one.

Layla attacked her lasagna with a knife and fork. He guessed she had reached one of the crunchy noodles. The action caught his eye and he studied her again. If he had met her before, would he have tried to kiss her? He smiled. The answer to that was a definite yes. He ran through several scenarios in his head, trying to decide which one he would have used on her, but came up dry. How could he know what would work on her when he knew nothing about her? They didn't even know why she was with them. Obviously she was in witness protection since their cousin was involved, but he hadn't given them any information about her case. What if she wasn't the one who needed protection? What if she was the one who had done something wrong?

He almost shook his head at the absurdity of that idea. She was sweet and good, of that much he was certain. His fists clenched in his lap. Had someone done something to hurt her? Was that why she had been sent to them? Didn't she have any family who was worried about her? She was only eighteen, after all. She had probably just graduated from high school, the same as him. If he suddenly went missing, his parents and brothers would go ballistic searching for him. Did her family know where she was?

He couldn't remember the last time he had been curious about anything. The sensation was a welcome change, making him feel half alive for the first time in ages. For so long he had simply existed. Time blended together, but he didn't try to mark it anymore. But now time had a new marker: before Layla and after Layla.

As he thought, he picked absently at his food, stopping only when his fork scraped plate. He looked down in astonishment. He hadn't cleaned his plate since the accident. What was it about this girl that was shaking him out of his stupor? He set down his fork with a clatter, not sure he wanted to be awoken. What was waiting for him but more heartache? His life had been determined months ago when he lost the use of his legs. At that moment he knew everything was over. He would never ride a horse again, never work alongside his brothers, never find a girl, fall in love and marry her. He swallowed hard. Never have children of his own.

Before his accident, he hadn't given a single thought to marriage and kids. They were what happened when a man became old enough to want to settle down with one woman. He was having too much fun to even begin to think in that direction. He liked being carefree. He liked being able to go out with any girl he wanted, whenever he wanted. He enjoyed the thrill of the hunt too much to give up the pursuit. Being tied down to one woman forever had seemed like a punishment.

But almost as soon as he woke up and realized he was crippled, his mind had turned in the direction of his future. Who would ever love him? Instead of being a rough and tumble cowboy, fully capable of providing for a family, he was now a burden to all who came near. He could only do the most basic things for himself. How could he inflict himself on any woman and, more importantly, what woman would want that sort of life?

Even if he somehow, miraculously, managed to find someone, what sort of father would he be? He couldn't play catch with his kids or teach them to ride a horse. Would he have to stay home while his wife worked? He couldn't tolerate sponging off his brothers for the rest of his life, let alone sponging off his wife. There was nothing he could do about his current situation because he had nowhere else to go. But he could protect some helpless female from being dragged down with him. No way was he ever going to fall in love or get married. Maybe eventually he would figure out what to do with his life, but it wouldn't include becoming anyone else's burden.

With that thought in mind, his eyes returned to his empty plate and stared blindly.

"Can I get you anything else, Cade?"

Layla's soft and pleasant voice saying his name caused him to look up again. Their eyes caught and held.

"What?" he rasped.

"Food," Coy said. "She's asking if you want more food."

He shook his head. "No, thanks. I'm good."

She nodded and broke eye contact when Coy said her name.

"I was wondering if you might like a tour of the ranch," he said. His peripheral vision caught sight of Cade and gave a half smile for his benefit.

Cade felt his old fighting spirit spring to life. Not this time, not this one. Coy could have all the town girls and all the vendor's daughters, but he wasn't going to kiss Layla, not if Cade could help it.

"She should go with Josh," Cade said, surprising everyone but Coy.

"Josh won't yammer in her ear the whole time exasperating her with his opinion on everything."

"Do I exasperate you, Layla?" Coy asked. He smiled and tipped his head to give her a better view of his dimple.

Cade rolled his eyes. His brother had practiced that move to perfection, and most girls fell for it. Not for the first time he cursed his lack of dimples. Girls love dimples for some unknown reason.

Layla, sensing tension and not understanding the cause, tried to be diplomatic in her answer. "I saw some cookie dough in the freezer. Who wants dessert?" She stood and scurried to the kitchen without waiting for an answer.

Cade laughed and clapped Coy on the back. "Better luck next time."

"Count on it," Coy said, and then he stood and followed Layla to the kitchen with his plate.

* * *

Fifteen hundred miles away, Max Stuart sat on a bench reading a paper. Neither Max nor Stuart was a name he was born with. He had long ago given up his birth names in order to form a new identity for himself. He liked to pretend he had forgotten his original name, but he hadn't. It was still tucked away in a corner of his mind, along with everything else from his childhood.

A smile played on his lips as he watched the doors to the Justice Department swing open and closed. No one knew exactly how many marshals worked from this office at any given time. The government dearly loved secrets, after all.

But Max loved secrets, too. He had enough of them for ten men, and he had the patience of a saint, if not the behavior of one.

Not for the first time he thought of the girl who had walked in on him last week as he was finishing a job. He wasn't usually so careless. How could he not have made sure the outer door was locked? He had been lulled into a false sense of complacency because the office was closed, but he should have known Mather would have some poor little dope showing up after hours.

He wondered if the girl was a foster kid. He rolled his eyes. Of course she was. No other girl would willingly go within a hundred feet of Mather. For a moment, he felt good about himself that he had saved the girl from having to deal with Mather. Then he smiled wryly. Too bad he had to save her, only to hunt her down and kill her.

Returning his attention to the newspaper in his hands, he surreptitiously watched and labeled everyone who came and went from the building. Marshals were as easy to spot as any cop. So far he had counted eighteen. There were probably a few more out on location, but even so the number wasn't overwhelming. He would watch them, learn everything there was to know about them, and then he would find the girl.

He smiled again, smugly this time. People were predictable. Cops were especially predictable. Somewhere one of these marshals was using a familiar safe house for the girl, probably with some obscure friend or relative. All Max had to do was sit back and wait to figure out which marshal was in charge of the case, and eventually he would discover a trail leading directly to the girl. Patience and diligence were required, but that was no problem, Max thought. More than one psychologist had labeled him with those very qualities. Of course, every diagnosis also ended with the word "sociopath" thrown in for good measure. He shook his head. Even psychologists were predictable.

He rattled his paper again and studied his horoscope, whistling happily when he read it was his lucky day.

CHAPTER 6

"I have an idea."

It was two days after the lasagna. The day before, Layla had tried to make a pot roast. Though all the brothers had made a heroic effort, she finally declared the charred mess inedible, threw it away, and baked some pizzas from the freezer. Now she sat at the breakfast table with Cade, nervously chewing her thumbnail and eying the freezers. She looked at him hopefully as soon as he spoke.

"One of our old cowhands does all the cooking when we go out to pasture for days at a time. He can teach you the basics."

She clasped her hands under her chin in a gesture he had come to recognize as hopefulness or excitement. "Do you think he would? I wouldn't want to take him away from his duties."

Cade laughed, something he had been doing with recurring frequency since her arrival. "Are you kidding me? He might fuss and say a bunch of nonsense about women's work, but his old joints will be thankful for a day off from the saddle. He's been with us for years, so we can't let him go, but we try to find light duty for him to do whenever we can. This will give him something productive to do and give Cam a break from trying to think up useless activities for him. There are only so many ropes to wind and saddles to polish."

"That would be great. Thank you." She beamed at him.

His heart stopped, then stuttered and started again. "You're welcome." He suddenly wanted to do whatever it took to make her smile again and keep her smiling. Before he could think of something, she spoke.

"Is your hair long on purpose?"

Self consciously, he pushed his hair out of his face. "No."

She bit her lip and studied her hands in her lap. "I could cut it for you, if you want." She peeked at him to gauge his reaction.

To her relief, he smiled in amusement. A part of him wanted to be embarrassed. His brothers hadn't commented on his long hair, probably chalking it up to his new, moody demeanor. He had no heart to tell them he was too embarrassed to go into town and have it cut. He hadn't been to town since the accident. If he had his way, he would never go again. But how could he be upset with Layla for guessing the secret when she looked as timid as a puppy asking permission to play?

"Do you know how to cut hair?" he asked.

"No, but I've seen it done. I could learn."

"So I'm to be your guinea pig?" he teased.

Her eyebrows knit together. "Or you could continue to let it grow and join a band, Samson."

He had never seen her vexed before. After a second of stunned surprise he laughed out loud. "You have a temper. Who knew?"

"Everyone has a temper," she said, trying hard to rein hers in so he wouldn't laugh at her again.

"Not Coy. You could punch him in the face and he would laugh it off."

She smiled. "Sounds like you speak from experience."

He grinned and nodded. "Want to try it tonight to make sure I'm not lying? I'll pay you ten bucks."

She giggled, imagining herself punching Coy. "Are you sidestepping the issue of me cutting your hair?"

He sobered and pushed his hair away from his face again. He desperately wanted it cut, but having her that close to him with her hands in his hair, well, he wasn't sure he could continue to keep her at arms' length after that. He opened his mouth to tell her no, but she leaned in, giving him a plaintive look.

"Please," she said. "I want to help around here. I want to feel like I'm doing something constructive with my time. Plus, I've always wanted to learn how to cut hair."

Did she know how appealing she was? If she did, she was a good actress. Rarely had he met a girl so unaware of her prowess, and he had met a lot of girls. Layla was at once capable and vulnerable, sweet without being saccharine, pretty without being stuck on herself, and kind without being weak. She was an enigma, and a lovely one at that. He was struck with the sudden desire to run his fingertip over her eyelashes. Were they as velvety as they appeared? There were no clumps of mascara marring their appearance, but how else did she make them so thick and dark? Surely no one was blessed with lashes so perfect.

"Okay," he found himself agreeing. "You can cut my hair."

For a moment she looked like she was going to throw her arms around his shoulders and hug him. He hoped and dreaded she would, all at the same time. But then she ran a subdued hand over her pant leg. "I'll need scissors and maybe some clippers. Do you have any clippers?"

He nodded. His mother had always cut their hair. The clippers were in the bathroom, along with the scissors. "I guess you don't snoop or you would know they're in your bathroom drawer."

"Or maybe I'm such a good snoop I'm feigning ignorance." She stood and sauntered down the hall, leaving him smiling in her wake.

She was good, but not so good she was boring. He found everything about her alluring, he realized. When she returned a few minutes later she had the scissors, clippers, and a spray bottle of water in her possession.

"A thought occurred to me as I was retrieving these. I don't know how you want your hair."

He shrugged. "Cut."

She rolled her eyes. "Men. I meant how did you wear it before? May I see a picture, please?" She held out her hand to him, palm up.

"I don't generally carry around old pictures of myself," he said.

She picked up the squirt bottle and misted him in the face. "Maybe you can tell me where to find one," she suggested.

He grabbed the squirt bottle, wrenching it out of her grasp. "Some people should never be given power. In the den are a whole bunch of photo books my mom assembled. Each one is labeled by name. Knock yourself out, but please don't keep me waiting forever."

She gave a longing look to the water bottle and he knew she wanted to squirt him again. He raised it and pointed it at her face. "Your time starts now. Hurry back."

She wrinkled her nose at him. "Some people should never be given power," she said.

He laughed and misted her backside when she turned away from him.

She felt unaccountably nervous as she flitted down the hall to the den. Not only did she not want to mess up Cade's haircut, but she didn't want her roaring attraction to him to become apparent. She had no idea how she was going to hide the truth of her feelings while standing so close to him, touching him.

But when she found the photo books, all thoughts of anything else fled from her mind. Picture after picture showed Cade strapping, robust, and cheerful. There were pictures of him on horses and with bulls. Some looked like they were taken at the county fair and most included scenes with his brothers. Undoubtedly they had been close and so similar as they worked the land together.

Unbidden tears sprang to her eyes as she studied one picture in particular. Cade stood by himself in the center of the photo. His happy, saucy grin dripped with confidence. He reminded her of Coy, only Coy was sweeter in nature. In picture after picture, Cade's smugness shone through. No wonder he was sad and surly these days. He was practically a shell of his former self. Now merely skin and bones, he had once been as well built as his brothers. His appetite for food, as well as for life, had been taken away.

A stray tear dripped on the picture. She used her finger to wipe it away. "I'm going to make you whole again," she promised. No matter what she had to do, she vowed to make Cade the man he had been in these pictures. She scrubbed her hands over her eyes, removing any trace of tears. Instinctively she knew he loathed pity and, truthfully, she didn't pity him. She was sad for him and for the life he had lost, but she understood something he didn't: he still had a whole lot of life to live. He simply needed someone to show him how and, for whatever reason, she believed herself to be that person.

By the time she returned to the kitchen, she was smiling and Cade was frowning. Only after he sent her away did he realize what he had done. She would see him as he once was; and then she would return and see him as he was now. How could she not be disappointed by the comparison? Then he had been whole and healthy. Now he was a broken invalid.

But when she entered the kitchen, she used his melancholy as a distraction. Lunging, she plucked the squirt bottle from his lifeless fingers and set it on the shelf beside her.

"Behave, or I'll use it again. Now that you know I'm capable of dousing you, I expect perfect behavior for the remainder of this haircut."

"Yes, ma'am," he said with forced meekness. In his mind, he grasped her waist and pulled her close, muttering something about teaching her a lesson. But before his imagination would let him kiss her, he was torn out of his daydream by the feel of her fingers running through his hair.

He closed his eyes and tried not to sigh. Except for the nurses who helped him maneuver in the hospital and his mother who hugged him goodbye a few months ago, he hadn't been touched since the accident. He had no idea he was starving for touch until he felt it again. How horrified would she be if he grabbed her, pressing his face to her neck in a crushing bear hug? Every fiber of his being was telling him to do just that.

On her end, Layla was having much the same thought, except it had been four years since anyone touched her in any way except aggressively. When she first entered foster care, she had been beaten up by another kid in the house. A couple of boys had grabbed her and she had been shoved a few times, but in all that time, no one had hugged her or held her hand, or even patted her on the back. She had tied up the part of her that longed for affection in a neat little sack. She had set it on a shelf in her heart and thought it was securely contained, but running her fingers through Cade's hair had the unfortunate and unsettling result of breaking open her secure little container. She wanted to be hugged and held and kissed and loved, and she wanted those things from Cade.

Before she could give in to her desire to fling herself at him, she made herself stop running her fingers through his hair. Instead, she picked up the scissors and started to snip. The cool plastic and metal of the scissors brought her a small sting of mental clarity. She took a few deep, steadying breaths and tried to get herself back under control again. Concentrating on what she was doing helped.

It was probably the longest haircut in history as first she snipped, and then used the clippers to trim, then clipped and trimmed again. Finally, she was finished. Only when she stepped back from him and set down the clippers did she realize his lips were pressed tightly together, and his face was pale as if he were in pain.

"Cade," she said softly. "I'm finished. Did I hurt you?" Had she inadvertently cut him or pulled his hair?

His eyes popped open and stared at her with intensity. He caught her wrist and held it. "Don't take a tour with Coy. I was serious about that."

Her brow puckered as she tried to follow his mental leap. "Okay," she drawled.

He relaxed slightly but didn't release her wrist. "Go with Josh. He knows a lot of the history of the ranch, but he'll only talk when you want him to."

She nodded, staring at his hand on her wrist. His thumb smoothed absently over the large vein right below her hand. "Why?" Her voice came out in a shaky whisper.

"Why what?" He looked at her unfocused, as if his mind was far away.

"Why do you want me to go with Josh instead of Coy?"

"Because Coy will kiss you," he said simply, as if that explained everything.

"And you don't want Coy to kiss me," she prompted, hoping he would continue.

"I," he started, but the side door banged open, interrupting him.

"Boss said you wanted to see me." It was their cowboy cook, Shorty. Cade had called Cam with the idea of having Shorty teach Layla to cook. As he had predicted, Cam was overjoyed with the plan.

"You're going to teach Miss Layla to cook," Cade said. "I have to go get cleaned up." He rolled himself from the room without a backward glance, leaving Layla to introduce herself to the leathery-looking cowboy.

CHAPTER 7

$\mathcal{C}$ade was suspiciously absent from supper that night, which was a shame because Shorty taught Layla how to make pot roast, and it was actually edible this time. She shoved down her irritation and put on a happy face for the remaining brothers, but inside she was seething.

She knew why he was missing. He was either embarrassed or repulsed by their earlier encounter. But nothing had happened. How had he taken an innocent touch to her wrist and turned it into some big thing? Did he think she thought more of it than it was? Was ignoring her his way of letting her down easily? If so, there was no need. She was used to rejection and solitude. She took the hint loud and clear; he wasn't interested. In the morning if things were still awkward between them, she would waste no time in setting him straight.

But he didn't show up in the morning, either. She slammed dishes and food around the kitchen for a while, and then she decided to go have it out with him. There was no telling how long she would be staying here. Better to clear the air now than to let things fester. Already, he had blown things out of proportion. Did he think she was so desperate for him that she would stalk him?

I'll clear up that misconception right now, she thought. She marched down the hall, wishing there was someone in her path she could shove out of the way. Not that she actually would shove someone out of her way; it simply made her feel better to imagine the possibility.

Raising her hand, she rapped brusquely on his door.

"Come in."

She frowned at his weak, raspy tone. Wary now, she peeked around the door and all her anger evaporated. His sheets were tangled around him, and even from across the room she could tell he was sick. His eyes were bright with fever when he looked at her with a combination of embarrassment and relief.

She strode to his bedside and pressed her hand to his forehead. It singed her palm. "How long have you been sick?" she asked.

"Almost since I left you yesterday. Why do you sound angry?"

"Because I am," she said. She straightened the sheets more comfortably around him, noting with relief that he was wearing flannel pajama pants. "I'll be right back." She exited his room and marched back to the kitchen. Banging cupboards, she finally located the glasses. She poured him a generous measure of juice, carried it back to him, and presented it like a bouquet of flowers by jutting it under his nose.

"No thank you," he said.

Her jaw dropped in astonishment. "Are you insane? You haven't had anything to eat or drink since yesterday, you obviously have a fever, and you're probably dehydrated. Drink."

"I can't exactly drink lying down, can I?" he snapped. "And I'm too weak to sit up." He turned away from her and faced the window.

With a frustrated sigh, she set the glass of juice on his nightstand with a thud. Then she leaned forward and put her arms around him.

"What are you doing?" he asked. He sounded panicked.

"Helping you sit up."

"I don't need your help." He tried to draw away from her, but she pinned him to the bed and looked into his eyes.

"Yes, you do. Shut up and let me or I'll get the spray bottle again." With some effort, she pulled him to a sitting position and plumped pillows behind him so he would be more comfortable. She held the glass of juice to his lips, but he brushed her hand away impatiently.

"I can hold the glass myself," he insisted, although when she let it go his hands shook with the effort. He drained the glass and set it on the nightstand then leaned back and closed his eyes. "That was good, thank you."

"Are you up to eating anything?" she asked.

He shook his head. "I'm fine, thank you."

She sighed impatiently again, causing him to open his eyes and look at her. "Are you actually not hungry, or are you trying to be macho again?"

He gave her a partial smile. "I'm starving."

"That's what I thought. Let me get a cool washcloth for your forehead, and I'll make you some toast."

He opened his mouth to protest, but she covered it with her hand.

"So help me, Cade, don't say another word."

He nodded and gave her a full smile this time. She retrieved a cool cloth from his bathroom. She bathed his face and pressed the cloth to his forehead before returning to the kitchen. There she prepared two pieces of toast with butter and jam. She also made warm tea and added a heaping teaspoon of sugar.

When she returned to the room, she thought maybe he was asleep, but his eyes opened as soon as she stepped through the door. He ate without comment while she refreshed his washcloth. She collected his plate, leaving the mug of tea because he was still sipping it, and walked back to the kitchen. After depositing the plate, she returned to his room once more.

"I thought you might like to go to the bathroom," she blurted, not knowing how else to say it.

"Please don't tell me you plan to help me in there," he said. He sounded slightly stronger than when she had first found him.

"I plan to help you get to there, but after that you're on your own." To her relief, she noted that his bathroom had been equipped with rails in the shower and beside the toilet, enabling him to care for his needs himself.

He opened his mouth, and once again she held up a hand to interrupt him. "Let me save you the trouble of telling me you don't need my help. I know you like to do things for yourself, and I appreciate that fact, but you're sick and weak and I don't plan to stand here and watch you struggle to save your pride."

He blinked at her, debating with himself about whether or not he was going to argue. At last the mutinous expression dissolved from his face and she knew she had won. He held out his arms for her. She leaned in and put her arms under his, pulling him forward as she moved backward. When she got him to the edge of the bed, she paused for a breath. He was much heavier than he looked. Although she had never seen him standing, she guessed he was about a foot taller than her.

The wheelchair was right next to the bed. With every ounce of effort she possessed, she somehow dragged him to it and kept him upright. When she finally stood and took a step back to wipe the beads of sweat from her upper lip, he was smiling.

"What's so funny?" she asked.

"You," he said. "I kept waiting for you to realize I wasn't helping you at all, but you never did. I've never had so much fun being helped out of bed before."

She put her hands on her hips. "You made yourself dead weight on purpose?"

He shrugged. "You wanted to help me, and the guest is always right."

"Just for that, I'm not pushing you to the bathroom," she said.

He rolled his eyes. "What dire punishment will you think of next?" He wheeled himself to the bathroom, which had been his aim all along. While he was brushing his teeth and washing his face, she changed the sheets on his bed. He had obviously sweated profusely in the night.

Guilt twisted in her chest. Previously, she had thought his pride kept him from appearing at supper last night. Turns out *her* pride kept her from checking on *him*. He had spent a miserable night alone for nothing.

He exited the bathroom looking weaker and paler than when he went in. "Are you sick to your stomach?" she asked.

He shook his head. "Just achy and feverish. My throat is sore." As if to emphasize his statement, he rubbed his throat and winced.

"You shouldn't be sitting up. Let me help you back to bed," she said.

"I don't want to lie in bed all day," he said.

"Cade," she began, but he interrupted her.

"I'll lie on the couch," he said. "Scout's honor."

"All right," she agreed. This time she took control and wheeled him down the hall to the den. What was so magical about this room, she wondered as she opened the door? Movement from outside the window caught her attention, drawing her eye. Outside, she saw Coy and Josh breaking in a new colt. Beyond, the cattle lowed and milled about in the pasture. She paused, staring out the window. His bedroom faced a small woods on the other side of the house. Did he love this room so much because it enabled him to see the ranch?

He began moving himself from the chair to the couch. By the time she opened her mouth to offer her assistance he was already on the couch.

"You are a very bad patient," she told him.

He grinned weakly before closing his eyes. His breathing was labored, and she felt a tremor of fear. Was he more susceptible to illness because of his handicap? What if whatever this was settled in his lungs and became pneumonia? He might die.

She brushed his newly shorn hair off his forehead. Shorter hair suited him better than long hair. For a first time, she thought she had done a bang up job. He hadn't said whether or not he liked it, but in retrospect he had probably felt too ill to give it much thought. After a few minutes he relaxed into the couch, and she knew he was asleep. Reluctantly, she left him and tiptoed from the room.

Shorty was waiting on her in the kitchen. As Cade predicted, he had grumbled about being sent to the kitchen to work, but she thought he was secretly delighted with the assignment. He puffed up with pride when she complimented him on his knowledge and experience. He relayed stories to her without her asking, but she was glad he did. They were interesting to her. He never asked about her, and she was glad about that, too. She didn't want to talk about herself. She didn't want to think about her life. Even though the reason for her being in Montana was horrific and scary, she never wanted it to end. More and more she felt accepted here. She wasn't a ward of the state, she wasn't a number. She was simply Layla, and she was learning that she liked Layla.

Halfway through her lesson, she paused and checked on Cade. He was awake and staring listlessly at the ceiling, but he turned to smile at her when she opened the door.

"How are you feeling?" she asked.

"Okay," he said.

"How are you really feeling?" she asked, knowing his bravado was false pride.

"Like the angels are coming any minute." He sank into the couch and closed his eyes.

"Can you eat anything?"

He shook his head and winced with the effort. "Juice," he murmured. "Or tea."

She left the room and returned with juice, tea, and a cool washcloth. After bathing his face and neck a few times, she pressed the cloth to his forehead.

"How is it possible to be cold and hot at the same time?" His teeth chattered and he sweated profusely.

"Maybe it's a good sign. Maybe it means the fever is breaking." She held the juice straw to his lips while he drank greedily.

"Or maybe it means death is imminent. Too bad you can't use the internet or you could look up the last stages of death."

"Haven't you ever seen a cow or horse die?" she asked.

"More times than I can count."

"Did it ever look like this?"

"No, but then I don't think any living creature has ever been this sick before."

She laughed, causing him to smile weakly. Although she was sorry he was ill, she was delighted he had dropped his pretenses and was being honest with her. That had to mean something, although she had no idea what.

"You shouldn't be near me," he said. "You might get whatever this is."

"I don't get sick," she told him.

"Famous last words," he said.

She waited until he finished the juice and then told him she needed to get back to the kitchen to finish supper.

He opened his eyes and looked at her in alarm. "You'll come back, won't you?"

"Promise," she said. "And if you're feeling up to it, I'll bring you some soup."

He grimaced.

"From a can."

He relaxed his expression.

"If you weren't so sick, I would make you pay for your lack of faith in my cooking abilities. Shorty is working a miracle in me."

"Can't wait to taste for myself," he said, and then he was asleep again.

CHAPTER 8

That night Layla relayed Cade's illness to his brothers while he remained asleep on the couch. None of them seemed concerned or upset over the fact that he had lain sick in his room for so many hours.

"He was alone for all that time," she reiterated.

"Cade likes to be alone now," Coy said with a shrug. "He doesn't like to interact or leave the house, so we leave him be."

Layla wasn't so sure. She was seeing the situation through fresh eyes and noticing things they didn't. Undoubtedly Cade was in a slump, but she wasn't sure that was the total cause for his antisocial behavior. He had reacted well when she asked him about his hair. Maybe she would be able to talk to him about the other things on her mind, too, although she would have to wait until he was better.

After she finished supper and cleanup, she retreated to the den with a bowl of soup and more juice for Cade. He was sitting up when she arrived, indicating that he had probably wheeled himself somewhere, most likely to the bathroom.

"I feel like I'm going to float away from all these liquids."

"It's important to stay hydrated when you're sick," she said.

"That's what my mom used to say."

She wrinkled her nose at him.

"Please tell me I didn't just compare you to my mom. Must be delirium from the fever."

"Must be," she agreed. She set the tray in front of him and arranged it while he watched.

"I feel wide awake after my five hour nap today."

"That's a good sign," she said absently.

"What I meant is that I'm bored and restless. Stay and watch a movie with me?" He patted the sofa cushion beside him.

She looked around in confusion. "There's no television in here, is there?"

"We'll watch on the laptop, unless you'd rather not?"

She hated the uncertainty in his voice. Why couldn't she have simply said yes instead of jabbering about the television? "I want to," she assured him. "Which movie?"

"You choose. They stream live, so you can get anything you want."

"I didn't understand most of the words in that sentence." She sat beside him.

He eyed her as he opened the laptop. "Were you raised Amish? Because you don't seem to have much of a relationship with modern technology."

"Not Amish," she said, but didn't elaborate.

He found the site he wanted and handed her the computer so she could select the movie.

"I'm conflicted because I really want to see a girly romance, but my conscience tells me to pick an action flick for you because you're sick."

"I've seen all the action flicks. Go for what you really want," he said. He would never in a million years admit that he had seen a lot of the girly romances, as well. She made her selection. It was one he hadn't seen. He pressed the button, set the laptop on the table and sat back. There was a moment of awkwardness as he tried to decide if he was going to put his arm around her. Realistically he knew he shouldn't, but it seemed like the natural thing to do. However, vanity took over and kept his arm in place. He hadn't showered since yesterday, and he had slept all night in a puddle of his own sweat.

Tension hummed between them, distracting them both from watching the movie. Eventually the plot caught their attention and drew them in. It was funny and sweet. Beside him she relaxed until he realized she was asleep. Her head lolled to the side and landed on his shoulder with a soft thud, but not even that woke her.

He used her slumber as an opportunity to stare at her unabashed. She resembled a china doll with her long lashes fanning her rosy cheeks. Her dark hair was mussed and splayed around her face, contrasting well with her porcelain complexion. His heart tapped out a staccato rhythm. Why did he have to meet her now when there was nothing he could do about it?

But if he had met her before the accident, he knew exactly what he would have done with her. He would have flirted with her until she gave in and went out with him, and then he would have dumped her. Back then he only cared about the pursuit, and not about the girl. Now he wanted to flog any man who would treat her as he once would have. His mouth twisted into a wry smile at the irony. When he was whole and capable of loving her, he would have used her most cruelly, never realizing the treasure she was. Now that he had more time to examine her heart and understand what made her so captivating, he was unable to love her and be loved in return.

Her lips parted slightly on a sigh. Over the years, he had kissed a lot of girls. But never had he wanted to kiss anyone more than he wanted to kiss Layla right now. There was something so sweet, compelling and womanly about her that he felt like he might go insane with yearning for her. Previously, he had dated girls and had crushes on them. Now those crushes looked paltry in light of what he felt for Layla, and the thought terrified him. His body was broken, never to recover. Would the same thing happen to his spirit when she left? Once again he marshaled his resolve. At all costs, he had to stay away from her. He couldn't get any more involved with her than he already was.

"Layla," he whispered.

She woke with a startled whimper, her eyes darting in terror.

"It's okay," he soothed, but she shrank back away from him. "It's me, Cade."

Immediately she relaxed and blinked up at him in confusion. "Cade." She repeated the name like a non-native trying to learn the language.

"Cade," he reiterated.

"I fell asleep."

"You missed the end of the movie."

"I'm sorry. Was it good?"

He shrugged noncommittally. He had missed it, too, because he was watching her.

"I should have warned you that I have movie narcolepsy. Turn on a movie, and I'm out. I'm not sure I've ever watched the ending to a movie."

"Maybe we should start in the middle next time." Next time? Was he insane? He was supposed to be getting away from her, not setting up future encounters.

She yawned sleepily, pressing the back of her hand to her mouth. "Can I get you anything else?" Unconsciously, her hand moved toward him and then hovered between them. She froze, searching his face. Was she looking for permission to touch him? He wondered what she read in his expression because her hand continued on its slow journey until it pressed against his cheek. Her thumb rubbed gently over his beard stubble. He closed his eyes and leaned in to her touch.

"Layla," he breathed, tilting toward her. And then the door opened, breaking the spell and causing them to jump guiltily apart.

"Well, well," Coy said. "I came to check on my poor, sick little brother. Looks like you're feeling better." He tried to infuse sarcasm into his tone, but in reality he was ecstatic to see some signs of life returning to his brother. He thought Layla was pretty, fun, and sweet, but if she was responsible for the recent changes in Cade, then he would have a brotherly interest in her and nothing more.

"I should go," Layla said. Her cheeks were pink with embarrassment. For once, Coy had the good grace not to goad her into further mortification. He stood aside as she swept from the room without saying goodnight to either man.

He turned from the door and raised an eyebrow at Cade. "So your record is up to fifty seven now? That puts me three girls behind."

Cade shook his head. "The record still stands at fifty six," Cade told him. He hefted himself into his wheelchair, his arms shaking with exertion. He hated being weak, and this bug had made him as weak as a newborn lamb. Add that to the fact that Coy had interrupted a delicate moment with Layla, a moment that should never have occurred in the first place, and he was in a roaring bad mood.

"From what I saw, your record will soon be broken," Coy said with his usual good humor.

Cade shook his head. "My record will never be broken because I'm tossing in the towel. You win by default. I never want to kiss another girl again," he lied. He didn't wait for Coy to move out of the way before he barreled by him, rolling over his toes in the process. To his satisfaction, Coy had taken off his boots so the wheels tread over his sock-clad feet. He howled in pain and most likely hopped up and down a few times, but Cade didn't turn to look.

He rolled to his room, dragged himself to his bed and fell into an exhausted slumber. For once he was thankful for the illness that kept him from replaying the torturous almost-kiss in his mind. There would be plenty of time for recrimination tomorrow.

CHAPTER 9

The next morning, his brother Cameron checked on him before he left for the day.

"Layla wanted me to see if you need anything," he said, poking his head around the door. "Are you feeling better?" There was no comforting warmth in Cam's tone, but Cade would have been disturbed if there was. His brother was almost robotic in his lack of emotion.

"I think I'm feeling up to par," Cade answered, trying to figure out if it was true. The fever was gone, but he was still weak. He didn't realize how much he had been looking forward to seeing Layla until she wasn't here. "Where is she?"

"Coy is taking her to town today. She left her home with barely more than the clothes on her back, and she needs things." Cam gave one of his controlled smiles. "You should have heard the argument she put up last night at dinner. She doesn't want to take anything from us."

"How did you convince her?" Cade asked.

"I pointed out that since she was cooking and cleaning for us she was technically our housekeeper and should earn a salary."

"And what was her reply?" Cade smiled in anticipation.

"She said if we were going to get technical about things she should start doing our laundry, too. I thought Josh was going to faint at the idea of a girl touching his underpants."

"But she won, didn't she?"

Cam nodded. "I would hate to be on the other end of a business deal with her. If her steely resolve doesn't get you, then her big doe eyes and long lashes will."

Cade looked at his brother in surprise. He had never heard him talk about a girl so, well, so normally. A prickle of apprehension wormed its way up his spine.

"Don't worry," Cam said. "I have no designs on your girl."

"She's not my girl," Cade insisted.

"Sure she isn't," Cam said. He closed the door and went back down the hall, leaving Cade to stew in his agitation.

If Cam thought he and Layla were together, then everyone must think so. Cam was always the last to know everything that didn't directly concern ranch business. After a few minutes of staring grumpily at the ceiling, his frown changed to a grin. Did it really matter if his brothers thought he and Layla were together? Even more gratifying to him than the thought of him and Layla as a couple was the fact that no one in his family seemed surprised. Did they think he could still get a girl? And if they did, did that mean he could? What if his disability was a bigger deal to him than it was to everyone else? Could Layla actually care about him in his current condition? Did he want her to?

The answer to that, he realized, was yes. But his newfound insecurities refused to be silenced. She hadn't seemed to mind helping him into his chair or taking care of him while he was sick, but that had only been one day. One day was very different than a lifetime. And she was only eighteen, like him. Eighteen was too young to know what she wanted for the rest of her life, wasn't it?

A new thought made him break out in a cold sweat. What if she had a boyfriend from wherever she was? Of course she did. She was practically perfect. Men must be falling all over themselves to get to her. She would leave here and forget all about the guy in the wheelchair. But she did seem to care about him. Was her interest genuine?

Back and forth his torturous thoughts swayed as he showered, dressed himself, and ate a lonely breakfast. The day was lonely, and that fact added to his irritation. He was no more alone than he had been before she arrived, why did he suddenly feel bereft? How had she come to mean so much to him in such a short amount of time?

At lunch, he stared across the empty table like a lovesick puppy. His behavior was ridiculous, and yet he couldn't help it. He missed her. That's when the most horrible thought of all struck him. She was spending the entire day with *Coy*. If he could have, he would have shot to his feet in indignation and panic. As it was, he sat back in his chair with a thud. Knowing his brother, he would make the trip last all day so Cade wouldn't have the chance to see her at all. He clenched and unclenched his fists. If his brother made a move on her, then so help him. Cade might be limited in his mobility, but he wasn't dead, and he knew Coy's weak spots.

For the remainder of the day, he comforted himself imagining some horrible torture for Coy if he dared to misbehave with Layla.

IF CADE COULD HAVE SEEN Coy with Layla, he would have realized all his worry was for naught. Coy behaved like a perfect gentleman. To his relief, he found it wasn't difficult to transfer his emotion for her to brotherly affection. He had worried that he wouldn't be able to take the chivalrous way out in order to leave things clear for Cade, but that didn't happen. Either his attraction to Layla had only been skin deep, or he loved his brother more than he realized. Whatever the reason, they had a pleasant day together as friends.

He did keep her out all day, but not on purpose. He was easily distracted and kept thinking of things he wanted to buy or show her in town. Several curious looks came their way. He tried to put on a show of keeping things light between them so no one would get the wrong idea. The town thrived on gossip. Sooner or later it was going to come out that she and Cade had a thing going. Coy had no desire to be in the middle of a love triangle with his brother, real or imaginary.

He gave everyone the story his cousin Jason had worked out, that she was their new housekeeper from the east. Knowing how much Shorty would gossip about the cooking lessons, he also added that she threw cooking in as a bonus. The last thing he wanted was for people to wonder why their housekeeper/cook needed cooking lessons from their oldest cowboy.

Jason hadn't given thought to the gossip her presence would cause in the town, Coy realized. A pretty young girl living on an isolated ranch with a bunch of cowboys was bound to cause talk. His only hope was that Layla's overwhelming sweetness and innocence would lay waste to any maliciousness. Their friends and neighbors, though curious, were basically good. Hopefully they would see the goodness in Layla and leave her alone.

Not for the first time he wondered why Layla was with them and where she came from. He was using uncharacteristic restraint by not prying into her life. Usually, he blurted whatever thought came to mind, including nosy questions. But there was something wounded about her that brought out his protective nature. He was reluctant to cause her any more trauma by reopening something that might be painful for her. What if she had watched her parents killed, or something horrible like that? She had never made mention of a family.

He eyed her as he drove toward home. There was no need to wonder what would happen to Cade when she left because Coy already knew the answer. What little spark of life was in him would be snuffed out completely. Somehow, he had to convince her to stay with them, but how? How could he convince her to remain with them when he had no idea where she came from or why?

He opened his mouth to try and ask her some questions, but found she was asleep. They were well out into the country now on roads that were as familiar to him as his hand, so he didn't worry about taking his eyes of the road to study her. She looked even more vulnerable asleep. How could anyone think of harming her?

After a few minutes he realized his heart was softening toward her a little too much. *Sister, sister, sister,* he chanted mentally. Gripping the steering wheel, he stared determinedly through the front windshield. Hopefully Cade would hurry up and stake an official claim on her, but who knew what thoughts went through Cade's mind these days? Despite the fact that Cam was his twin, Coy had always felt closer to Cade. They were more similar in personality and interests. It had been difficult to see him reduced physically, but seeing his spirit diminish and fade away felt like a death. Of course no one knew how hard Coy was taking the accident because he kept his negative emotions to himself. There was enough sadness and despair in the world without adding his own. But he felt it, just the same. He glanced at Layla, once again saying a silent prayer of thanks for her. If she could bring Cade back to them, he would hogtie her to keep her here if he had to.

* * *

If Coy had been able to read Layla's mind that day, he wouldn't need to devise ways to try and keep her at the ranch. While she was having fun with Coy, she didn't understand the feeling of melancholy stealing over her. She wasn't normally such a home body, why did she feel like she wanted nothing more than to get back to the ranch?

Maybe it was because no place she had lived in the last four years had felt like home. She had moved from foster home to group home so often over the years that she lost track of how many places she had lived. The state provided her with one bag, and all her possessions fit into it. No matter where she lived, she always had the same small piece of real estate consisting of a single bed. Nowhere had ever felt inviting. She was one of those rare individuals who couldn't wait to wake up and go to school in the morning. She loved her school locker because it was all hers and it actually locked. At "home" she always had to be mindful of her possessions or they would come up missing.

But now she had a room all her own, and a bathroom to match. She was beginning to organize the kitchen the way she wanted so it would be easier for her to find things. She had learned the best settings on the washing machine, and she knew the coziest, most comfortable spot in the den. More than that, though, there was a sense of belonging that had nothing to do with physical space. She fit in with the brothers. She was learning to love them in vastly different ways. No matter where she went she would never forget them, and the more time she spent with them, the less she wanted to go.

Staying was impossible, though. They were a family with wealth and land. They had no need of an interloping female. She could never learn to cook or clean well enough to become indispensible to them. Anyone with a broom and oven mitts could take her place. Instead of hoping for what might be, she resigned herself to what was. Eventually she was going to leave this place. She would trade in majestic mountain landscapes for government slums and smog. The best she could hope for was that the newfound skills she was acquiring would be enough to help her find a job when she got back. If she did a good enough job, maybe she could use Cam as a reference some day.

She tried to cheer herself with that thought, but failed miserably. Having a job and being able to support herself was a lofty goal, but it felt hollow because she would once again be completely alone. With that dismal thought in mind, she rested her head on the window and fell asleep.

CHAPTER 10

*C*ade was nervous when he woke the next morning. He hadn't seen Layla since their almost kiss the day before she went to town. Would things be awkward between them today?

But when he wheeled himself into the kitchen, she wasn't there. His brothers stood looking at each other in dismay as if they didn't know what to do with themselves without Layla to take care of them, as if they hadn't been taking care of themselves for the last year since their mother moved away.

"Where is she?" Cade asked.

"I don't know," Coy answered.

"Did you upset her yesterday?" Cade asked, his voice tight.

Coy shook his head. "No, nothing like that. We had a fun day. She fell asleep on the way home and I carried her to bed. I left her clothes on," he added, seeing Cade's mutinous expression.

Cade hadn't been thinking of her clothes, though. He had been thinking that he would never be able to carry Layla anywhere. It was a cruel reminder of his limitations that increased his bad mood.

"Maybe she's sick," Josh suggested. "Someone should check on her." All eyes turned to Cade.

"Why me?" he asked, knowing full well the answer was because they had all deemed her as his girl and therefore his responsibility.

"Because we're all going to work," Cam said.

His reasonable logic did nothing to dim Cade's ill humor. Already sensitive this morning, it felt like a jab to his wounded pride. He would go to work with them if he could. Sensing his bad mood, they filed quietly out the door.

Cade jammed his wheelchair into reverse, spinning so fast he almost dislodged himself. He angrily wheeled down the hall to Layla's room, but when he knocked on her door his fury turned to concern.

"Come in," she rasped.

When he pushed open the door he saw what she must have seen when she found him in his room two days ago. She lay shivering and sweating in a pile of tangled sheets, her already pale face almost ghostly white.

"I thought you never get sick." He rolled over to her and tried to pretend he wasn't panicked at the sight of her dark-circled eyes and dry lips. Had he sounded this raspy when he was sick?

"You're gloating now, really?" she asked weakly.

"No, I'm not." He picked up her hand and clasped it in his. His panicky feeling returned when he realized he had no idea what to do with her. He had never taken care of someone who was sick before. What had she done for him?

"Juice," he muttered. "I'll get you some juice."

"I can get it," she said. She pulled herself to a sitting position and closed her eyes when the room swam.

He grasped her shoulders and pushed her back down. "You're going to be a worse patient than I was, aren't you?" She nodded. "Lie still. I'll be back in a minute." He couldn't fit his chair into her bathroom, so he rolled down the hall to his bathroom and wrung out a wet cloth, returning it to her. She sighed in relief when he pressed it to her forehead and settled the blankets more tightly around her shoulders.

"Back in a minute," he said again. He wheeled down the hall to the kitchen, retrieved juice and put on a pot of tea, trying not to think how much faster he could do everything if he wasn't confined to a cumbersome chair. By the time he reached her room with the juice, which he had spilled as he bounced down the hall, the tea kettle was whistling. Suppressing a sigh, he returned to the kitchen, poured the tea and then stared at it in consternation. How was he supposed to get boiling hot tea to her without scalding himself?

Inspiration struck. He retrieved a lidded to-go mug and poured the tea into it. The contents sloshed a little, but didn't spill over. When he reached her, he remembered that she had made him toast.

"Do you want toast?" he asked.

She shook her head.

"Do you really not want toast, or are you trying not to be a burden?"

She smiled weakly. "I'm really not hungry, thank you."

"Do you want to go to the den?" he asked.

She shook her head. "Too weak to make it."

He pressed his lips together, angry with himself once again. If he was whole, he could easily carry her down the hall to the den.

"Stop it," she commanded gently.

"What?" he asked. Could she really know what was on his mind?

"You're angry because you can't carry me," she said.

"How do you know?" he asked.

"I just do," she said. "But you're taking care of me fine." She reached out and clasped his hand.

"I could have done it better, before." He brushed her hair off her face, noting how hot her forehead was.

"Would you have?" she asked. "Would you have missed a day of work to stay home and take care of me?"

He opened his mouth and snapped it closed again. How did she know? Of course he wouldn't have missed work to take care of her. He loved his work on the ranch. He might have called one of the women from town to stay with her, but he wouldn't have done it himself.

"How did it happen?" she asked. She held her hand in both his and studied his face with wide, fevered eyes.

He scraped his bottom teeth over his top lip. Talking about the accident was always painful, but he wanted her to know everything. "A bull and I had a disagreement. The bull won. He stepped on me, snapping several vertebrae and partially crushing my spine. I won't walk again."

"I'm sorry," she said.

Her eyes held sympathy, but no pity. Although he appreciated it, he didn't understand how it was possible. To his way of thinking, any girl in her right mind would either pity him or be repulsed by him. Layla seemed to feel neither of those things. He had a not so sudden need to know and understand her.

"What's your last name?" he asked.

"Smith."

"Is that an alias?"

"I wish," she said.

"Why?"

"It's too easy to get lost in the system when your last name is Smith."

What system? Why would she get lost in it? He wanted to know everything about her, but she was too sick to plague with questions. One more and he promised himself he would stop.

"Where are you from?"

"Chicago. Before this, I had never been outside the city."

"What do you think of the country?" He held his breath. Some city-bred people could never let go of their love for city life. Chicago was huge. Was she bored here?

"I love it. Feels like home," she murmured, and then she fell asleep.

She woke when he returned with lunch a few hours later.

"I brought soup," he announced. She regarded him with questioning eyes. The soup was located on a high shelf. Perhaps someday he would show her the long pole he had tethered together from several barbecue forks, but not today. "Want me to feed you?"

"What do you think?" she asked. She took the spoon off the tray, raised herself to a sitting position, and began to eat.

"I think you're not very good at being taken care of," he said.

She finished her soup in silence, too weak to make a reply. When the bowl was empty, she pushed back the covers. "I want to brush my teeth, take a shower, and change my clothes."

"No shower," he said. "You're too weak."

"But," she began. He interrupted her with a shake of his head.

"You're bossy," she complained. She swung her legs to the floor and sat swaying for a few seconds. He leaned forward and held out his hands to steady her.

"Sure you're up for this?"

"As ready as I'll ever be," she said.

He leaned closer and cinched his arms around her in order to pull her to a standing position. She overbalanced and they both fell backwards against his chair. She propped her arms against his chair and tried to push herself away.

"What's your hurry?" he asked. They were very close together now, face to face.

"I'm grubby," she said miserably. Why when he finally decided to make a move on her did she have to be sick and gross?

"I'm a cowboy. I'm used to grubby girls."

"How used to grubby girls are you?" she asked.

He grinned wickedly. "Very."

Jealousy gave her the strength she needed to push away from him and stalk to the bathroom. When she emerged slightly cleaner but still rumpled, he was still smirking in amusement.

The sight of her bed made her grimace. She couldn't stomach any more time in there for awhile.

"I think I want to go to the den now," she said.

"Lean on my chair while I roll," he said. She did as he said, leaning heavily against the chair as she shuffled down the hallway. They reached the den and she collapsed onto the couch.

He lifted himself from his chair and sat beside her.

"Tell me I'll feel better tomorrow," she said wearily.

"You'll feel better tomorrow."

"If I'm still alive then," she said.

Even though she was sick and exhausted, he still wanted to hold her. "C'mere," he said, reaching for her.

She shrank away. "I'm," she started, but he interrupted.

"You're grubby, I know. I don't care."

Her eyes narrowed. "That's right; you have plenty of experience with grubby girls."

He chuckled, putting his arms around her and pulling her close. "You're too sick to waste energy being jealous."

She nestled close to him, reveling in the warm comfort of his embrace. "True. Remind me later and I'll pick up where I left off."

"There's no way I'm agreeing to that." He ran his fingers through her hair. "Do you have a boyfriend in Chicago?"

"No." Her tone was dreamy because nothing had ever felt as good as being this close to him. It was almost worth the horrible virus if this was the end result.

"Did you?" he asked.

"Did I what?" She had already forgotten the thread of the conversation.

"Did you have a boyfriend?"

"Not recently," she said. She was too embarrassed to tell him she had never dated anyone. "When was your last grubby girl?"

"Around the time of my accident a year ago."

His tone was angry, alerting her that something bad must have happened between him and the girl. "What happened?"

"Nothing, at first. We hadn't been serious before the accident, so I was surprised when she continued to hang around. She visited me faithfully every day at the hospital. Then I found out she was enjoying a little bit of celebrity on my behalf. After every visit, she reported on every aspect of our conversation, my care, my state of mind and prognosis."

She winced on his behalf, sure he had hated so many people knowing details about him.

He was amazed and gratified that she understood him so well. Impossibly after such a short time, she *knew* him. Even more amazing was that she had seen him at his worst and still seemed to like him.

"What brought you here?" he asked.

She tensed. He smoothed his hand up and down her arm until she relaxed again. "I saw a murder."

He froze. "What happened?"

"I exited an elevator, opened an office door, and saw a man exit the office holding a gun. Behind him, I saw the man he had killed." For her own sanity, she made the tale as clinical as possible, leaving out the fact that she had been going to the office to meet Mr. Mather.

"How did my cousin get involved?" he asked. The guy who was murdered had to have been high profile for Jason to put her into witness protection.

"The murdered man worked for the state, but he did some consulting work for the federal government. They took over the case and, voila, Marshal Wright brought me here." She shuddered, swallowing down the fear she refused to think about.

He clutched her tighter, swallowing down his own impotent rage. He wanted to find the killer and make sure he didn't harm her, but of course he couldn't. There was nothing he could do to protect her and that thought worked to cool some of his ardor.

"Want to watch a movie?" he asked. He released his grip, but couldn't quite let go of her completely. His arm remained behind her on the back of the couch.

Undaunted by his mercurial mood shift, she smiled up at him, causing his heart to squeeze painfully. "Sure, but you choose. I have the feeling I'll be asleep by the opening credits this time."

He made his selection and, true to her prediction, she was asleep by the time the movie started. Her hunched position looked uncomfortable. He pulled her toward him so she was lying down with her head pillowed on his leg. She slept fitfully, whimpering and jerking as if she were having nightmares. He wanted to wake her for his own peace of mind, but knew she needed the sleep.

He left her to eat supper with his brothers.

"Layla's stuff is already better than this," Coy said as he poked at some scrambled eggs he had made for them. "I think she's going to turn out to be a really good cook." He glanced at Cade. "Has she said anything about staying?"

"I haven't asked her," Cade replied.

"What's stopping you?"

Cade tried to rein in his impatience with his brother. If Coy felt something, he said it. If he wanted something, he acted on it. That way worked for him, but Cade was more subtle about things, especially since the accident that robbed him of his confidence.

"I barely know her," he said, which was true. Although he knew the fundamentals, like the fact that she was funny and sweet, he knew none of the facts of her life.

"Better hurry up and get to know her," Coy said.

"Don't rush me," Cade said. "And what makes you so certain I'm going to ask her to stay, anyway?"

The brothers dropped their forks and looked at him.

"Don't you want her to stay?" Josh asked. He was always the one who cut through the chase and got to the heart of the matter.

There was a pregnant pause while Cade did battle with his pride. After spending his life wild, it wasn't an easy thing to admit to his brothers that he had finally been tamed. "Yes, I want her to stay," he bit out.

"Don't sound so happy about it," Cam said.

He wolfed down the remainder of his food in silence, anxious to get back to Layla. Knowing her, she would wake and try to walk down the hall on her own, and she was too weak for that.

Josh carried a supper tray and juice glass for her. When they arrived back at the den, she was beginning to stir. She gave them a sleepy smile that sent his pulse racing. Maybe they were only eighteen, but he was pretty certain he could wake up to that smile for the rest of his life and never grow tired of it.

"Thanks, Josh," she murmured, causing his cheeks to pink as he tipped his hat and backed out of the room. She turned her attention to Cade. "How was the movie?"

He shrugged one shoulder. After watching every movie known to man the last few months, he had lost his zeal for them.

"You're tired of watching movies," she guessed.

"How do you know? How do you know these things about me?"

Her index finger trailed a circle around the juice glass. "I've always been an observer," she said. "But somehow I just know. It's like I have a pipeline into your thoughts and emotions." She quirked an eyebrow at him. "Creepy, huh?"

"In theory," he agreed, but he had felt that same connection to her from the first moment he looked into her eyes. "How are you feeling?"

Now it was her turn to shrug one shoulder. "Okay."

"The truth," he prompted.

"Like the angels are coming any minute," she said with a sigh. She set the juice glass on the tray and leaned back against the couch. She closed her eyes, remembering.

The last time she had a virus was two years ago. She had been living in a terrible placement at the time with a family who only wanted her for the money the state provided. They barely fed her, let alone clothed her or cared for her in any way. She had spent as little time there as possible, even when she had that horrible illness. She went to school, propping her tired eyes open and attempting to cool her raging fever with drinks from the water fountain. At last one of her teachers had noticed her fever-bright eyes and sent her to the nurse.

The nurse had scolded her for coming to school when she was obviously so ill. She called the foster family, but they never showed up to collect Layla. Instead, she had spent the remainder of the day sleeping in the nurse's office, and it had been one of the best, most relaxing days of her life. She hadn't had to worry about being attacked in her sleep. She had slept the sleep of the dead, the same way she had slept since she arrived at the ranch. Even though a killer was after her, she felt safe here.

Cade pressed his palm to her forehead, checking her fever. She opened her eyes to look at him, so close to her face. He gave her a gentle smile and tucked her hair behind her ear. Her emotions were always too close to the surface when she was ill and now was no exception. She felt tears brimming just below the surface of her eyes and worked to push them back down.

"Thank you for taking care of me," she whispered.

He rested his head on the back of the couch and studied her. "Who takes care of you at home when you're sick?"

"No one," she said, too weary from her illness to be evasive. "No one has ever taken care of me."

She could see the questions swimming in his eyes. He wanted to know about her, but she didn't want to tell him. How could she? His life wasn't perfect, but it was a far cry from hers. He had parents and brothers who loved him, a home that was his, and every creature comfort money could buy. She had none of those things, but it was more than that. She was too familiar with the looks people gave her when they learned the truth about her.

Over the years, she had gone to more schools than she could count, and it was always the same thing. At first, kids looked at her with open curiosity and friendliness. And then some teacher would unknowingly out her as being a foster kid, and it was as if someone hung a flashing light and sandwich board around her neck that announced her as an outcast. Being a ward of the state had made her an exile the last four years, and before that her home situation did the same thing. Here she had finally found acceptance because they knew nothing about where she came from, they only knew *her*. There was absolutely no way she was going to do anything to jeopardize that, even if it meant keeping the details of her life from the one person who was beginning to mean the most to her.

"I'm sleepy again," she announced, cutting off any opportunity for him to ask questions. It was true, though; she was inexplicably tired again.

He put his arm around her, drawing her gently to his side. He pressed a light kiss to her temple. "Sleep, then," he said, and by the time he finished speaking she was already out.

While she slept, he sat in silence, thinking. None of his thoughts were new, but they were still so wondrous he wanted to examine them again.

Her presence in his life was nothing short of miraculous. Just a couple of weeks ago, his life had been a dead end. He had been sure he would never love and no one would ever love him. He had resigned himself to living out his life alone. His bitterness and frustration knew no bounds.

And then Layla came along.

She refused to accept his gruff rejection of her. She saw through his angry façade to the lonely guy underneath. She made him laugh again. She made him hope again.

But, like always, his thinking was circular; it always returned to one pressing question: was it fair to inflict this life on her? She was beautiful, young, and vibrant, full of hope for a bright future. Why should she be encumbered with a crippled hermit as a companion? Eventually the newness of what was between them would fade, and then what would be left? How long before she began to resent the fact that he never left the house? How long before she started to yearn to go on dates like other girls her age?

He sighed wearily. Her arm slipped over his waist and hugged. He smiled. Even in her sleep, she sensed his emotions and tried to comfort him. She was his miracle, how could he let her get away? He would have to make some changes, even if it meant bending his pride to do so.

That thought was still foremost in his mind when Coy poked his head in to grin at him sometime later. For whatever reason the sight of Cade with Layla seemed to either please or amuse his brothers, especially Coy.

"Goodnight," Coy whispered.

"Goodnight," Cade replied. He wanted to leave it at that, but his newfound resolve wouldn't let him. "Wait," he called.

Coy pivoted in the doorway to face him.

"She's still too weak to walk down the hall, and I don't want to wake her. Maybe you could carry her." Saying the difficult words was like spitting glass. *He* wanted to be the one to carry her, but that was impossible.

Coy grinned at him and waited while he hefted himself into his chair before leaning over and picking up Layla as if she weighed no more than a sack of flour. *I used to be able to do that, too,* Cade thought, with no small amount of bitterness and yearning. He started to wheel himself toward the door, but now it was Coy who called him back.

"Wait," he said. He leaned over and deposited Layla in his lap before positioning himself behind the wheelchair in order to push them both down the hall.

To Cade's immense satisfaction, Layla put her arms around his neck and nestled her face against his chest. She hadn't done that with Coy. Was it possible that she somehow sensed his presence in her sleep? He wondered over that possibility on the too short trip down the hallway. He wheeled her to her bed and watched as Coy lifted her from his lap and onto the bed. He left Cade to arrange her covers and together they backed out of the room.

CHAPTER 11

For the second day in a row, Layla awoke in her bed with no idea how she got there. And for the second day in a row, she looked down in relief and realized she was still wearing her clothes. But her relief quickly turned to disgust when she realized she had been wearing the same clothes for two days now.

Gingerly, she sat up. The room swam a little, but when her vision cleared she realized the illness was gone with only slight weakness lingering in its wake. She took a long shower, scrubbing everything twice to try and remove the feeling of being grubby.

The word "grubby" made her think of Cade. Smiling, she hummed to herself as she finished getting ready. He had no idea how unusual yesterday had been for her. She hadn't been exaggerating when she said no one had ever taken care of her before. In her early life, she had been the caregiver. Once she entered foster care, she looked out for herself. Now that she was feeling better, the feeling of being cared for almost overwhelmed her. She tried to listen to the rational side of her brain because it told her yesterday had been no big deal. If anything, it had been repayment of a debt. She took care of him when he was sick, and then he took care of her.

But her emotions ran wild with the memory. For years she hadn't belonged to anyone, hadn't been loved by anyone. Instead of becoming hurt or angry over the circumstances of her life, she had bundled all her wanton emotions into a well-secured package and placed that package in the far-reaches of her heart, never to be examined again. When another foster kid was adopted instead of her, she didn't allow herself to feel hurt or rejected. When kids at school made fun of her for living in a group home, she refused to feel the pain of their torment. When teachers sent home forms for parents to sign and she had to have her social worker sign them, she didn't allow herself to feel humiliated.

The problem, she now realized, was that she had trained her heart to deal with negative emotions. Rejection, abuse, loneliness, cruelty and abandonment all bounced off her hardened outer shell. But love, care, friendship, and romance were cracking the impenetrable façade she had worked so hard to construct. She had no idea there was a chink in her armor because no one had shown her any kindness in all those years.

For that reason, when she was finally ready, she didn't go to find Cade. She bypassed the kitchen, stepped outside, and went in search of Cam.

Luckily for her, he was in the ranch office and not out on the range today. He looked up in surprise when she knocked on the door. She had barely left the house since her arrival, and this was her first time setting foot in the office located next to the main barn.

"Layla, is something wrong?" Cam asked solicitously. "Are you still sick?"

She shook her head. "I wanted to talk to you about something."

"Go ahead." He held out his hand, indicating the chair across from his desk.

She sat and twisted her hands nervously in her lap. "Cade doesn't leave the house," she said.

Cam blinked at her. "I know."

"But do you know why?"

"Because he's depressed and he doesn't want to be among people,"

Cam said. He, along with Coy, was hoping her presence would fix that problem.

Layla shook her head. "That's not why. It's because there are three porch steps."

Confusion was still the predominant emotion on his face. "We would gladly help him down those. He knows that."

"Of course he does," Layla said. "He knows you would do anything for him. But he doesn't want you to. He wants to do everything for himself."

"But that's not possible anymore," Cam argued.

"I know. Eventually he's going to have to make some concessions and learn how to take help. But there are still a lot of things he can do for himself. I know I'm an outsider here, and it's not my place, but sometimes an outsider with a fresh perspective can see things more clearly than someone who has been living in the situation."

"What, exactly, are you saying?"

"He needs a ramp," she said.

Cam sat dumfounded, thunderstruck by the simplicity of her idea. Why on earth hadn't they thought of a ramp? Could that really be the reason Cade hadn't left the house since the accident? Had his pride kept him prisoner because he didn't want to ask one of them to wheel him down the steps?

Yes, that was exactly why. He knew because he would have had the same problem. They all suffered from too much pride.

"We'll get started on it right away," Cam said. Plans, costs, and materials began ringing in his head, providing a welcome distraction from any emotion.

Layla beamed at him. "Thanks, Cam. I knew you would jump on board as soon as you understood the problem."

He gave her one of his oddly controlled smiles. She wondered if he had ever guffawed in his life. "Are you sure you can coax him outside once the ramp is built?"

She nodded. "In fact, I think once it's done I'm going to have a hard time getting him to come back in again."

He grinned at her. "I hope so. We all miss him out here."

Not as much as he misses being out here, she thought, but didn't say it. There was no need to belabor the point. She thanked him once more and bounded back to the house. Now that she had done something for Cade, she felt the playing field was more level. Perhaps it wasn't romantic to keep track of who did what for whom, but that was how she felt most comfortable.

He sat at the kitchen table, worrying a napkin between his fingers. He looked up at her when she entered, a guarded expression on his face. "Are you okay?" His tone was wary, cautious.

Her happiness over the thought of the soon-to-be ramp turned to euphoria at the sight of him. "I'm great," she said. "Did you eat?"

He shook his head, still regarding her with wary eyes. She giggled because her behavior was puzzling him. The only breakfast food she knew how to make, thanks to Shorty, was French toast, and so that's what she made.

"This is good," Cade commented. "I think Coy is right. You're turning into a good cook."

"You and Coy have talked about me?" She gave him what she hoped was an innocent look.

He smiled, returning her falsely innocent stare. "Wouldn't you like to know?"

Yes, she would, and she wanted to know everything they said. But saying so would make her appear needy, so she simply smiled and let it go. She stood to clear and wash their dishes while he watched her.

"What's on the agenda for today?" he asked.

"I need to strip the beds, do some laundry, vacuum the carpet, and probably scrub the kitchen floor. Oh, and Shorty is coming for another cooking lesson. We're making beef stew today."

"Wrong."

"No, really, I just ran into him on my way back in the house and that's what he said we're making."

"I meant you're not doing all that other stuff. You're still too weak."

She waved a soggy hand in front of her face dismissively. "I'm fine."

"You're forgetting I'm a day ahead of you in virus recovery. I'm just now back to full strength. Take it easy today. Please," he added as an afterthought.

She looked at him over her shoulder, wrinkling her nose, but he knew he had won. "I'm still going to cook with Shorty."

"I was hoping you would. I love beef stew. But the other stuff can wait."

"I suppose," she agreed.

"You don't have to do any of it, you know," he said. "You're our guest."

She finished with the dishes and dried her hand on a towel, shaking her head. "Someone who stays for a couple of days and doesn't do anything to help out is okay. Someone who stays for… however long I'm going to be staying, well, the point is that I need to do something to feel like I'm not mooching off you guys." She tried to walk by him to grab the broom, but he caught her wrists.

He held them together like handcuffs, forcing her to stand before him. "We want you here. Jason offered us a stipend for keeping you, but we refused it."

She blinked at him, unable to disguise her sudden tears. "You did?"

He nodded and frowned. "Why are you crying?"

She shrugged and tried to squirm out of his grasp to wipe her eyes. He shifted her wrists so they were held in one of his hands, and used his free hand to wipe her eyes. She knew he was waiting on an explanation, but she didn't want to give him one. Without divulging her entire history, there was no way to tell him that the only reason anyone had ever taken her in before was because they were being paid to do so. No one had taken her because they wanted her. But the news, while happy, made her all the more determined to earn her place here. Today she would acquiesce because he wanted her to take it easy, but from tomorrow on she would work twice as hard. She would make the house perfect, the food perfect, everything perfect.

Unfortunately, her resolution did nothing to stop her helpless tears. It seemed that once loosed they refused to be stopped up again.

"Layla, please don't cry," he rasped. "I…it hurts me."

Her tears came to an abrupt halt when he said that. Apparently even her tear ducts wanted to please him and keep him from pain. "Okay," she said, sniffling a little.

He grinned. "Wow, that worked. Go make me a banana cream pie," he commanded.

She remained standing in place, although she was smiling now.

"I guess you need some fine tuning before you follow all my commands," he said.

She was catching her first glimpse of the smug, cocky charmer he had once been. He sat back in his chair, smirking. His sudden burst of conceit brought out a flirtatiousness in her she didn't know she possessed. She leaned forward, resting her arms on the chair.

"Maybe you're not asking in the right way," she purred.

He took a second to recover from his shock and then he grinned and reached for her. She dodged him with a laugh and ran down the hall toward the den.

"No fair," he yelled after her. "I'm handicapped."

"Wheel faster," she yelled back.

He laughed, loving the fact that she spared him no pity.

CHAPTER 12

The brothers started on the ramp that very day. Cade, alerted by the hammering, rolled to the window and stared out.

"What are they doing?" His tone was agitated, most likely because he felt left out. Men were outside working with power tools and he was inside, teaching chess to a girl.

"Sounds like they're building something," Layla said calmly.

"I know that, but what? We haven't discussed any renovations. Ranch business decisions are supposed to be shared. No one asked me." He tapped his finger impatiently on the window.

Layla knew she shouldn't, but she was enjoying his irritation. Especially because she knew he was going to feel like a heel when he found out that what they were building was for him.

"Maybe they had a meeting while you were sick," she told him, knowing full well she shouldn't goad him.

"They could have waited." He turned stricken eyes to her, and her amusement faded.

"Cade, it's probably minor. They would never do something important without consulting you. You know that, don't you?"

She watched as the irritation and hurt faded from his eyes. Finally he smiled at her. "How do you do that, Layla?"

"Do what?"

"Talk me down that way. I've always been the one with the worst temper. I can't tell you how many times I've gotten in trouble because I acted first and thought later. But you say a few words and it's like I magically see everything differently."

She shrugged. She didn't think she had done anything special. He turned his attention back to the window.

"Checkmate," she announced.

He spun in his chair to study the board, incredulous. He laughed at what he saw. "You can't jump me. This isn't checkers."

"Someone's a sore loser," she said.

He wheeled over to her. "Someone is clueless. Let me explain the rules. For the fourth time, but who's counting?"

She tried to listen attentively while he tried to teach her again, but the words ran together and sounded like gibberish. A teacher had also once tried to teach her chess. It hadn't made sense then, either. This time it could have been because while he talked she stared dreamily at his face. How did he keep his beard stubble at exactly the same, perfect length every day? She knew he did it on purpose because the pictures she had found before the accident showed the same perfectly even amount of growth.

"How do you do that?" she blurted.

"You take the bishop and you…" he began, but she interrupted him.

"No, not that. *That.*" She pointed to his face. "How do you keep the stubble the same length every day? It defies the laws of science."

He grinned. "Beat me at chess and I'll tell you."

She growled in frustration. "I'm no good at chess."

"You could be if you actually listened to me when I tried to tell you the rules. I can tell you're zoned out."

"And yet you continue speaking." She pretended to snore.

There was a small, round table between them. He shoved it away with a sweep of his arm. "Now you're in trouble," he said.

She squealed and dashed from the room before he could catch her.

By the time he rolled to the hallway, she had already reached the kitchen. "Someday I'm going to catch you, and when I do I'm going to kiss you," he called.

Shorty poked his head around the corner of the hall at him. "Then I'll have to learn to run faster," he said, sending Layla into a fit of giggles behind him.

* * *

Far away in Chicago, Max Stuart prepared for an early dinner with an accommodating and ugly woman. He chuckled to himself as he buttoned his cufflinks. Ugly women were so easily manipulated. Did they never wonder why a handsome, wealthy, sophisticated man was suddenly attracted to them when no man had ever been attracted to them before?

Long ago he had learned that every woman wanted to be a princess, complete with her own Prince Charming. So he made himself that man and, POOF, women became putty in his hands. Without fail, he could eventually get any information he wanted from them.

This one was a little more cunning than most. She fancied herself as the main character in a Jane Austen novel. While her witty observations were sometimes amusing, her overall intelligence was tiring. On their first date, he had made the mistake of asking about her job. She had blinked at him, owl-like, and said something vague. After that, she remained suspicious, and he'd had to back off any inquiries about her work.

But now, several perfect dates later, she was starting to relax completely. Unbidden, she had let slip a few facts about her job. Nothing classified, of course, but enough to show him she was beginning to trust him.

From his own observations, he had already narrowed down the possible list of candidates to two people who might be handling the witness protection case. One was a female agent named Charlotte. She was an unattractive, masculine-looking woman who resembled a bulldozer in both form and personality. Normally, he hoped his intended victim was a woman because he had certain charms that never failed to work on the fairer sex. But in this case he knew he would get nowhere if he tried to romance Agent Charlotte.

The other possibility was Agent Jason Wright. Over the years, Max had learned that people's interests and activities often showed up on their bodies. Dancers, for instance, moved with a lithe gracefulness. Swimmers had the unconscious habit of swinging their arms, as if they were warming up to dive into the water. And horse people, well, they swaggered. He didn't yet know much about Jason Wright, but one thing he knew was that he had spent a lot of time on a horse. He intended to find out where and when, just like he intended to find out everything about agent Charlotte, including her last name.

But not tonight. Tonight he had to have yet another perfect date with the ugly, witty woman. Soon, though, he was going to start asking some questions, and he was going to do it so well she wouldn't even realize she was giving him the answers.

* * *

BACK IN MONTANA, the four brothers and Layla were just finishing their beef stew.

"That was delicious," Cam said. Everyone else agreed.

"I've had Shorty's beef stew before," Coy said. "And it has nothing on yours. I think you're a natural."

She smiled at him. Shorty was showing her the basics, but she was developing her own taste for how things should be. She thought the stew needed more spices, so when his back was turned, she threw some in, along with a few other things.

The brothers excused themselves and went back outside. A few minutes later, their hammering began again. She smiled at the door until she noted the look on Cade's face. Maybe it was a mistake to keep the ramp a surprise. Maybe they should have told him what they were up to.

"I have something for you," she said. He looked at her with questioning, melancholy eyes. "Shorty taught me how to make a dessert today." She stood and scraped her chair back from the table. She went to the refrigerator and returned with a banana cream pie. She set it before him and started to retrieve plates, but he grasped her hand to stop her.

"Forget plates," he said. He picked up his fork, dove into the pie and held out a bite for her.

"You're giving me the first bite of your favorite dessert?" she asked.

He nodded. "A sign of how much I care."

"Or a good test to make sure it's edible," she said.

"You'll never know which," he said, shoving the forkful of pie between her lips.

They sat feeding each other forkfuls of pie, talking and laughing until late into the night. When they went to bed the other brothers were still outside.

CHAPTER 13

There was a tap on Layla's door. Her eyes popped open and stared blearily at the clock. It read five AM, an hour before her usual wakeup time.

"Layla, it's done," Coy whispered.

She sat bolt upright, threw off the covers, sprinted to her door and threw it open. "It's done?"

"It's done," he repeated. He looked exhausted and he was wearing the same clothes as the last time she saw him.

"Did you work all night?"

He nodded. "When the King brothers attack a problem, it gets solved," he said. His self-aggrandizing statement was ruined by a face-splitting yawn.

She smiled. "And kill themselves in the process, apparently."

"Yes, ma'am," he agreed and yawned again. "Come look." He clasped her hand and tugged her behind him. He opened the outside door and pulled her through, but then held her back. "You can't walk on it. The paint's not dry."

She put her hand over her mouth and laughed because, not only was there a perfectly built ramp on the front of the house, but also one on the back, and they were both painted. "You guys." She threw her arms around his shoulders and kissed his cheek. "You're the best."

"It was your brilliant idea," he said, sounding sheepish for once.

"Who cares?" she said. "I could never have built something like this in a day. It's perfect. He's going to love it. I'm going to make us a huge breakfast." Now she was the one who tugged his hand and pulled him behind her.

He yawned. "Later. I'm going to catch a few winks before we get started for the day. Cam said we could sleep until six."

She laughed and shook her head. Normal people wouldn't be able to accomplish twelve hours of ranch labor on an hour of sleep, but the King brothers weren't quite normal. "Then I'll cook while you sleep." She squeezed his hand. "I know you didn't do it for me, but thanks all the same."

He squeezed her hand and returned her smile. "It was a little for you. What makes you happy makes Cade happy."

Her eyes filled with tears.

"Ah, geez," he said. "I'm too tired to figure out if those are good tears or bad."

"Good," she whispered, swiping them away. Her emotions were really out of control lately.

He nodded. "Catch you in an hour."

She stood watching him go, then crept to the den and turned on the laptop. Her heart was racing at the prospect of being found online by whoever was looking for her, but Cade had assured her that as long as she didn't sign into any sites that registered her name she was anonymous.

When the computer booted up, she found a recipe for cinnamon rolls and printed it. Cinnamon rolls were ambitious, but they were one of her favorite foods and she wanted to make them as a celebration.

"Well, well." She spun to see Cade sitting in the doorway. He was dressed, but he looked untidy and disheveled as if he had hastily thrown something on.

"I was using the computer to search for a recipe." Her earlier computer-laden guilt sprang to the surface with his accusing tone. He wasn't actually angry she was using the computer, was he?

"That's not all you've been using, apparently."

"What are you talking about?" She was completely baffled by his angry, injured tone.

"I heard you get up. Thinking you might be sick, I lifted myself out of bed and went to check on you. Imagine my surprise when I saw you kissing my brother."

She snorted a laugh and put her hand over her mouth to try and stop it. She knew she shouldn't laugh at him, but he looked so cute with his messy hair, rumpled clothes, and angry expression.

"You think it's funny?" he asked, almost shouting.

"Shh," she said. "Your brothers are sleeping."

His fists clenched on his wheelchair. "Let me tell you something," he began.

She held up a hand to halt him. "Don't. Stop right there before you say something you'll truly regret. Take a little while to cool off and we'll discuss this later after I make breakfast." She smiled and plucked the recipe off the printer. "I'm making cinnamon rolls," she announced cheerfully. She brushed by him, ruffled his hair and laughed when he shrank away from her touch.

She was insane. There was no other explanation for it. First she had pretended interest in him while secretly sneaking around with Coy. And then, when caught, she had acted like it was all a big joke. She was diabolical. She was...not upset. Why wasn't she upset? Shouldn't she have shouted at him in return? Girls who enjoyed jealousy also enjoyed drama. Where was the drama?

He scowled at the opposing wall as he tried to puzzle things together. Playing him and Coy off each other wasn't something Layla would do, and neither would she laugh at him when confronted with her treachery, but what explanation was there?

He sat staring at the growing light outside, feeling sorry for himself. He should have known better than to let down his guard and allow her to worm her way into his heart. This was his punishment for being stupid. Lesson learned, it would never happen again. He was through with girls and romance. And Coy.

After awhile, his brothers began to stir. The smell of freshly baked cinnamon rolls assaulted his nose and made his mouth water. No matter how good they smelled, though, he had no intention of giving in and going to breakfast where he would have to see not only Layla, but his two-timing, back-stabbing brother, Coy.

The door opened. "Come on."

Cade grimaced. It was Cam. "No," he said, standing up to Cam for the first time since he was a little kid. Cam was the boss, that fact was undisputed. The three remaining brothers rarely bucked him because he was almost always right.

"Yes," Cam said. He came over, disengaged the brake on the chair, and wheeled Cade down the hall to the kitchen.

Cade sat silently while cheerful conversation swirled around him. He refused to touch the cinnamon roll Layla plated and set before him, even though it smelled and looked delicious and his brothers were exclaiming rapturously.

"Let's all go outside," Layla said brightly as soon as they were finished. She clapped her hands together excitedly.

Cade looked at her like she was insane, which she probably was.

"No," he said belligerently.

She nodded her head at his brothers and they descended on him, pushing his chair through the door while he tried to apply the brake. Once outside they all stopped and stared into the yard. It took a minute for the red haze to disappear from his vision enough to be able to see the long ramp in front of him.

"What the…" He cut himself off, too shocked to know how to finish.

"Layla had the idea that you might like to get outside now and then," Coy said, his laughter barely contained. Layla had filled him in on Cade's jealous tirade in the den. "So we worked all night long to get one done. Oh, and there's one on the front of the house, too."

Cade blinked at the ramp. To his horror, he felt tears sting the backs of his eyes. "Thanks," he said, his voice husky.

There was nothing like emotion to make men scatter. "Work," Cam announced, and the three brothers disappeared.

After taking a moment to compose himself, Cade looked at Layla. She had her arms crossed over her chest, glaring at him.

"Do you have something you want to say to me?" she asked.

He nodded and with a lightning fast movement reached out and grasped her waist, pulling her onto his lap. She screamed and tucked her head against his shoulder as he took off down the ramp at full speed. They glided to a stop at the bottom where she still sat trembling.

"How did you know you'd be able to stop?" she muttered against his chest.

"I didn't," he said. He cupped her cheek and pushed her head back so he could see her face. "I'm an idiot."

"We agree on that point," she said, a little breathless at the unbidden ride down the ramp, as well as his proximity. Her hand caressed his cheek. "You want to know how to make it up to me?"

He nodded, staring at her mouth.

"Tell me how you keep your beard stubble the same length all the time."

He threw back his head and laughed, startling a chicken into flight. "Fine. I don't keep it this way. I shave every day and a few hours later this is what I look like. I sprout hair like a yeti."

She giggled and rested her head on his shoulder, looking up at him.

"Now it's my turn to tell you what I want," he said seriously. He caressed her cheek with the back of his hand.

"What?" she whispered.

"I want to go back into the house and devour all the remaining cinnamon rolls, and then I want you to make another batch because I don't think what's left on the table is going to be enough for me."

She laughed and pushed off his lap. Together, they went back up the ramp and into the house.

* * *

LATER THAT NIGHT, Cade lay on his floor exhausted and angry.

He had just done sit-ups and push-ups, a hundred of each. They were the first ones he had done since the accident. There was a good chance his muscles would be too sore to be able to move tomorrow, and he still had to somehow pull himself back into bed, but that wasn't why he was angry.

"Cinnamon rolls," he muttered, pounding his balled up fist on the carpet. He'd had the perfect opportunity to kiss Layla and instead he had said he wanted cinnamon rolls. What was wrong with him? She hadn't seemed offended, but who knew what she was thinking behind that mysterious smile?

Why *hadn't* he kissed her? He had never passed up an opportunity to kiss a girl before. In fact, his previous philosophy had been to kiss first and ask questions later. But Layla was different. He was different now, too. What they had together was special, and he didn't want to blow it by pushing too far, too fast.

He didn't want to say he was afraid but, who was he kidding, he was scared out of his mind. An actual relationship with someone he cared about was new territory. Even before the accident, he wouldn't have known how to proceed. Previously, his modus operandi had been to do what he wanted, when he wanted, and hope the girl was along for the ride. But now the stakes were higher, the highest. Layla was perfect; the kiss would have to be, too. Hopefully when the next perfect opportunity came along he wouldn't blow it.

CHAPTER 14

The next day, Layla's prediction about Cade came true. He left the house immediately after breakfast and had to be coaxed to return for lunch. Cam told them he had plans to put in a sidewalk that would run from the house to the barn and office, but for now Cade seemed content to wheel himself around the yard.

"Let me push you," she said when they went back outside after supper. He had stayed outside while she cleaned and cooked supper with Shorty, and she knew his arms had to be tired from so much pushing.

"I'm fine," he insisted. "I stopped being able to feel my arms after the second hour out here."

She laughed and took over pushing duties. It was no easy task, even though the yard was leveled due to years of heavy traffic. "Where do you want to go?"

"The barn. I want to show you something. Keep going until I tell you to stop."

She pushed him to the barn, through it, and out the back. "Stop," he said. He positioned himself facing the western horizon. "Want to watch the sun set with me?"

"Yes." Before he could pat his lap for her to sit down, she ducked into the barn and retrieved a plastic chair, dragging it behind her as she reemerged.

He frowned at the chair, holding it responsible for the distance between him and Layla. How was he supposed to kiss her now, scoot his chair closer to hers and lean over until they met in the middle? No way. Instead, he contented himself with reaching for her hand and twining their fingers together. She gave a contented little sigh that made him smile.

She scooted her chair closer to his to narrow the distance between them and laid her head on his shoulder. "It's beautiful here."

"The most beautiful place in the world," he agreed. For two months after the accident, he had lived with his parents in Arizona while he recovered. His mother hoped to make the situation permanent, but he missed home. Reluctantly, she had let him return with the hope that the beauty and familiarity of Montana would work to draw him out of his black mood.

But as much as he loved the ranch, it had done nothing to cheer him. He had felt even more isolated and useless as he watched his brothers working busily in the yard from his prison window. And then Layla came, freeing his heart and freeing his body from the confines of the house. Breathing the fresh, familiar country air once again made him feel euphoric.

He turned to look down at her and saw her looking up at him, a tender look on her face. It never failed to amaze him that she actually seemed to like him as much as he liked her. What did she see in him but a worthless kid confined to a chair?

His effervescent joy at being outside again wouldn't let him sink into melancholy. And then it hit him: this was his moment. They were alone. The sun was spectacular with shades of pink and purple that covered the entire vast horizon. Layla was only a breath away and looking up at him like she wanted nothing more than to kiss him as much as he wanted to kiss her. He closed his eyes and leaned toward her, but suddenly she wasn't there anymore.

She had sat bolt upright, and was looking around the interior of the barn. "Did you hear that?" She continued on without waiting for a response, which was good because he had none. Did she not realize she was the one who had spoiled the perfect moment this time?

"I heard a cat meowing."

He blinked at her in dismay. "Probably. We have a million of them."

She gasped and clasped her hands together under her chin. "You do? Do you think there might be kittens?"

"There are always kittens," he said.

She stood so fast the plastic chair toppled to the ground. "Can I find them?" Again, she didn't wait for an answer before darting into the barn.

"Sure," he said lamely to himself. After one, wistful look at the perfect sunset, he wheeled himself into the barn.

He suggested places for her to look while she rooted around in the hay, searching for hidden kittens. After his initial disappointment, he got into the spirit of things and began suggesting obscure, out of the way places where kittens would never be. She scrambled up and down ladders and stumbled upon three nests of mice before finally catching on to his game.

She came to stand before him. Her hands were on her hips and she wore a stern expression, but the effect was ruined by the clumps of straw sticking out of her hair.

"You're cute when you're irritated and covered in hay," he told her.

"Cade, I'm like the Incredible Hulk. You don't want to see me angry."

He laughed and pointed to the corner of a horse stall. She took a step, then paused and looked back at him. "Is this another trick?"

He shook his head. "One cat always has her kittens there. Check and see."

Sure enough, as soon as she poked her head over the stall, she gasped and began exclaiming over their cuteness. He had no idea what the big deal was; he wasn't exaggerating about their massive army of cats. But when he saw the soft, adoring expression on her face as she peered at the cats, he had a new appreciation for them.

"Take one out and pet it," he said.

"Can I?" she asked, her tone wistful. "The mom will still take care of it if a human touches it?"

"What on earth do they teach you in the city? Of course she will. Pick one up." He watched while she climbed over the stall. He could have teased her by pointing out that she was climbing over the door instead of opening it, but he was too enthralled by her extreme excitement over the kittens.

She retrieved a tiny gray fur ball and came back to him, sitting in his lap without waiting for an invitation. He put his arms around her, cuddling her close as she exclaimed over every feature of the kitten.

"I take it you've never had a cat before," he said.

She shook her head. "I've never had any pet before, but I love animals."

"This one will be yours, then," he said.

She looked up at him, tears swimming in her chocolate brown eyes. "Do you mean it?"

He nodded. Why did she cry over the simplest things? She wasn't one of those girls who put on an emotional display over everything. Most of the time, she was calm, cool, and collected. But a few times, certain things did had made her cry. He wracked his brain, trying to remember them. He felt that if he could make the connection, he might be able to find some insight into what made her tick.

The kitten attached the claws of all four paws to her shirt and promptly fell asleep. "Oh," she gasped. "It's so adorable." She looked up at him again, smiling this time. Their eyes met and caught, and everything froze.

This was it- his moment. *Don't blow it,* he warned himself. He cupped her cheek with his palm and leaned down, eyes closed, and then stopped.

She opened her eyes and looked at him in question.

"Riders," he said. The word was meaningless to her, but he pointed toward the large door of the barn in time to see Coy and Josh ride in and dismount their horses. Sensing a private moment, they ignored Cade and Layla, but it was too late. The moment was shattered. Cade tried to find comfort in the thought that there would be a hundred such moments with her; he simply had to be patient.

He distracted himself by watching his brothers unsaddle and curry their horses. Those actions were once as familiar to him as breathing, but he hadn't done them in so long he wondered if the curry comb would feel clumsy in his hand.

As Cade watched his brothers with the horses, Layla watched him. What must it be like to be a rancher unable to ride a horse? The thought of what he must be feeling made her sad. She stood and unsheathed the kitten from her shirt. "I think I'll go inside," she said.

He started to follow, but she stopped him. "Stay," she commanded. "I know you're enjoying the fresh air. I'll see you tomorrow." She kissed her fingertip and pressed it to his lips, belatedly remembering that she had also touched a newborn kitten and baby mice with that finger.

Cade frowned at her backside as she walked away. Was she angry with him? Why else would she leave him so early? But, no, if she had been angry she wouldn't have pressed a kiss to her finger.

"Women," he whispered. He would never understand them.

"Amen to that," Coy said, hanging his saddle on the wall.

"What's wrong with women?" Josh asked. "I think they're nice."

"If you have to ask, then you wouldn't understand the answer," Cade said. He and Coy began laughing, and then laughed harder at Josh's confused expression. Josh was as innocent as a baby lamb, and Cade didn't want him to change any time soon. Even though he and Coy had dated multiple girls by the time they were sixteen, he wasn't anxious for Josh to follow in their footsteps. Josh was a steady, forever sort of person. Cade guessed he would only date one girl in his life. She would be the one he was with forever, and sixteen was too young for forever.

So is eighteen, a cynical little voice reminded him.

Shut up, he told that voice.

INSIDE, Layla tip-toed to the den, wondering if she would ever get over feeling like a criminal for using the computer. Using her favorite search engine, she found what she wanted and spent a long time doing some research. Instead of printing anything out, she copied notes on a piece of paper, then folded it and tucked it in her pocket. Smiling to herself, she walked down the hall, went to bed, and promptly fell asleep.

CHAPTER 15

The next morning found her once again sitting in the ranch office across the desk from Cam. This time she closed the door because there was a good chance Cade could be outside, and she didn't want to be overheard.

"What can I do for you today, Layla?" Cam asked. Was that amusement she heard in his tone, or exasperation?

"I was thinking," she began. He sat back and templed his fingers under his chin, waiting for her to continue. "Wouldn't it be great if Cade could ride his horse again?"

"Yes, it would," he said, his tone cautious. "If it were possible, we would love that."

"Oh, it's possible," she told him. She pulled out the piece of paper from her pants pocket and laid it between them on the desk. "Did you know there are specially made saddles for paraplegics? I don't know much about saddles, so I'm not sure what the difference is, but I wrote down some things for you to look at." She slid the paper to him.

He scanned the paper and said, "Hmm," occasionally. At last he set it aside. "Sounds good. I'll buy one."

"Just like that?" she said. The saddles were expensive, so she had prepared several possible arguments in case he didn't see things her way.

"Just like that," he said. "Was there anything else?"

"Nothing I can think of right now," she said.

"I'm sure you'll let me know the minute something else pops into your head."

This time she was sure he was making fun of her, even though his tone was even and he didn't smile. "The very minute," she said. He surprised her with a short burst of laughter that died almost as soon as he let it out.

When she exited the office, she found Cade sitting at the horse corral, watching the men work. Before going to him, she retrieved her kitten and sat on the fence near his chair. They sat in silence for awhile, watching the foals cavort with each other. He reached out and grasped her calf, sliding his hand under her jeans to caress her ankle.

"You need boots," he commented absently.

"Then you wouldn't be able to do this," she said.

"You make a good point. Still, a girl on a ranch without boots is like…" He paused and gave a rueful look at his chair. "Is like a guy on a ranch in a wheelchair. Very out of place."

Since she was seated above him, she draped her leg over his shoulder. "These other girls you mentioned, did they all wear boots?"

"Maybe," he said. He snaked his hand up to the sensitive area behind her knee. She was glad she remembered to shave that morning.

"Are you trying to fit me into their mold?" She was only half teasing.

He turned to look up at her. "No. I'm trying to acclimate you to ranch life. It's no place for tender toes." He tapped her toes for emphasis. "There are snakes, and rocks, and horses that clomp on feet. Boots make sense out here."

"But not in Chicago," she said, looking out over the horizon and shading her hand over her eyes to avoid the sun's glare.

He frowned up at her. "Have you heard something from Jason that makes you think you'll be leaving soon?"

She shook her head, hating to think about going back to the city, much less talk about it. "No, but it's a reality. Eventually I'll go back."

His frown deepened to a scowl. She sounded so certain; was it because she was dying to get back? Did she miss her sophisticated city life that much? The thought left him cold. He removed his hand from her leg and faced forward.

"I suppose," he said sullenly.

Now it was her turn to frown. She looked down at the top of his head, puzzled. Why did he sound like going back to Chicago wasn't a foregone conclusion? That had been the plan from the beginning and it was too much to hope it would change. Besides, no one had mentioned anything different. At night she dreamed that the brothers asked her to stay on and be their housekeeper, all except Cade, who asked her to stay for a better and different reason.

But while she was awake, time marched on and nothing changed. Allowing herself to get her hopes up would be masochistic. She was going back to Chicago, and that was that.

They sat in awkward, tense silence until it was time for her cooking lesson with Shorty, and then she went inside.

The quiet tension continued through supper. Coy, Josh and Cam picked up on the simmering undercurrents between Cade and Layla and remained quiet, unwilling to make things worse. Everyone was relieved when the meal was finished. Layla began to clean the kitchen while Cade went back outside to the barn.

"What's up with you two?" Coy asked, trailing behind him.

Cade sighed as he came to a stop in front of the horse corral. Once upon a time when he was upset, he would have thrown himself on his horse and ridden until his anger burned itself out. Sitting beside the horses and watching helplessly while they frisked around the corral only added to his futile frustration.

"I don't know," Cade said.

"What do you mean you don't know? How could you not know?" Coy pressed. Not only did he want things to work out for Layla and Cade for their sakes, but he was beginning to have selfish reasons for wanting her around. The food and house hadn't been so nice since their mother left.

"I mean I don't know," Cade exploded. "She seems bent on returning to Chicago."

"Have you asked her to stay?" Coy asked. He propped one arm on the fencepost and leaned at an impossible angle to take the weight off his aching foot. Earlier, a pregnant cow trounced on his foot. If not for his boot, the foot would have broken. As it was, he had a raging purple bruise that throbbed every time his blood pulsed.

"No, I haven't asked her to stay," Cade said.

"Why not?" Coy said.

"Because it's not that simple," Cade replied.

"Why not?" Coy repeated.

Cade looked at him in exasperation. The intricacies of a relationship were apparently very simple for an outsider looking in. "Because I don't know what's waiting for her in Chicago. I don't know if keeping her here is keeping her from something better there."

"So ask her," Coy said.

Cade clenched his fists. "I can't just ask her that. And besides, she doesn't tell me things." He frowned as he realized the truth of his words. Layla didn't seem closed off, but she was awfully good at telling him nothing personal. When he tried to gently probe about her life, she turned the conversation around so they ended up talking about him. To his chagrin, he realized now how much time he had spent talking about himself. After so many months of self-imposed solitude, he was relieved to have someone he could talk to. The consequence of all his soul-bearing, though, was that she knew everything about him, and he knew nothing about her. He didn't like that; he didn't like that at all.

"Well you're going to have to figure it out pretty quick," Coy said, crossing his arms over his chest. He stared down at Cade imperiously from his superior height. Cade had always been an inch taller. Secretly, he believed Coy was a little bit thrilled with the height advantage Cade's wheelchair gave him.

"You have all the answers, don't you?" Cade asked.

Coy grinned, impervious to his brother's temper. "Yes, and it's about time you realized."

Cade rolled his eyes. "Tell you what: When you get a girlfriend who keeps you up nights making you crazy because you don't understand her, then you can feel free to give me advice."

"So she's your girlfriend," Josh said, coming up on his other side.

Cade blew out a breath. A hundred thousand acres and he couldn't find a breath of space from his interfering family. "I don't know, we haven't discussed it," he said.

"Why not?" Josh asked.

Coy sputtered a laugh, and it was the last straw for Cade. He wheeled himself back inside, rolled to the den, and slammed the door.

* * *

IN THE KITCHEN, Layla winced with the slamming of the door. Usually, she didn't have to guess why Cade was upset. She had an uncanny sense about the things that made him angry or sad. For Cade, sadness was also conveyed through anger. In fact, his most prevalent emotion was anger. She was learning to look behind his angry façade to see which emotion he was actually feeling.

But now he was angry with her, and she had no idea why. Was he truly angry, or was his anger a cover for some other emotion? If so, what was it? What had she done to set him off? She thought back to their earlier conversation at the corral.

Everything had been going well until she mentioned Chicago. She sat up in alarm. Was that it? Did he not want her to go back? Her heart beat faster with that thought. Undeniably, there was something between them and, most likely, the thought of her leaving was painful to him. Maybe he wanted her to stay, but didn't know how to ask.

For a few minutes, she let herself feel euphoric at that thought. But then her hopes quickly sank and died. Even if Cade wanted her to stay, there was no way she could. All of the family would have to agree, and why would they? Just so she and Cade could carry on their relationship, whatever it was? Why would Cam, Coy, and Josh want an interloping girl from Chicago in their midst just because their brother liked her? There was no reason. How awkward would it be for them to explain her presence to *their* girls? She had never had any girl friends for that very reason. In her experience, girls were jealous and territorial. The guys wouldn't want their dating style cramped by their erstwhile housekeeper.

Once she hit on this brilliant solution to Cade's anger, she determined to make it better. Maybe he wasn't angry with her at all; maybe he was angry with his brothers because they didn't want to keep her. Or maybe he was angry with the situation in general because of its futility. She didn't think it was possible he was angry with her. Why should he be? She hadn't done anything wrong.

But if he was angry with his brothers, he shouldn't be. They were entitled to their own lives and opinions. They weren't obligated to keep her here. They had already done enough on her behalf. In fact, they had gone to extremes to make her comfortable, even giving up reimbursement for the money she cost them with her presence. She hated being the cause of enmity between them. Brothers shouldn't let anything come between them, especially not a houseguest.

With that thought in mind, she marched down the hallway to the den, determined to remedy the problem, not realizing that she had misconstrued the entire situation. The problem she was about to try and fix was imaginary, and her attempts were about to make things much worse.

CHAPTER 16

Standing outside the den, staring at the door, Layla was suddenly nervous. "Cade." She said his name softly and tapped the door.

"Come in," he said.

She opened the door and saw him as he had been the very first day she arrived—staring sullenly out the window. She sat on the couch and patted the seat beside her. He didn't turn to look, but he must have known what she was doing because soon he turned his chair and rolled over to her.

She waited while he moved himself from the chair to the couch and then did what she wanted to do the first time she saw him sitting so lonely and sad in this room; she put her arms around him and hugged.

He rubbed his stubbled cheek against her smooth one, enjoying the contrast, and then pressed his face to her neck, inhaling deeply. She smelled good. Had there ever been another girl like her? Not in his life. He rolled his eyes at his thoughts. He was turning into a girl. If his brothers heard his lovesick ramblings, they would take away his man card.

Her fingers twined in his hair, causing his heart rate to increase even more until it became a painful throb against his chest. She was in his arms. They were alone. This was his moment. He pulled away slightly to have better access to her lips. She stared at him with her big brown eyes, opened her mouth, and spoke.

"Please don't be angry with your brothers."

He blinked at her, trying to figure out what she might be talking about. "What?"

She eased away from him, twisting her hands nervously in her lap. "It's not their fault."

"What's not their fault?"

"The fact that I have to go back to Chicago."

Had he missed something? He looked behind him at the door, trying to remember the last thing they had said to each other. What was she talking about? "What?" he tried again.

"Everyone has been so nice, and so welcoming, but we knew it couldn't last."

He continued staring at her, trying to assimilate her meaning. Was she breaking up with him? Not that they were actually together, but still. Her words had the ring of finality. "Oh."

Oh? That was all he had to say about her looming departure? Maybe she had misconstrued things. Maybe he didn't care all that much that she was going away. Maybe he would be relieved to have her out of his hair. She edged farther away until there was a physical space between them.

Sensing her withdrawal, he faced forward and stared gloomily out the window. If that was how she wanted it, then so be it. He mustered his last scrap of pride and put on a happy face. "You'll probably be glad to get back to the city where you're more comfortable." With her friends, family, and guys who weren't confined to a chair.

So it was true, he was anxious for her to go back to the city. Why else would he sound so cheerful about it? To her horror, she felt tears prick the backs of her eyes. She would not cry, but she needed to make a quick escape unless an errant tear bucked orders and escaped down her cheek.

"I think I'll turn in early." Thankfully, her voice remained steady, revealing none of her inner turmoil.

He nodded, but otherwise didn't reply. As she stood and filed past him, she had the desperate hope that he might grab her waist, pull her back, and kiss her, but he didn't. He didn't speak, didn't touch her, didn't even look at her. Only a lifetime of practice suppressing her emotions kept them intact now.

Cade waited until the door closed before he released his pent up sigh. How had he misread her signals so completely? He thought she cared. He thought they had something special. But in her mind, she was ticking off the seconds until she returned to Chicago. He had always been a country boy, but never had he resented the city more than he did right now. Maybe if Montana had more culture or sophistication to offer Layla, she wouldn't be so anxious to leave.

He swiped his hand wearily over his face. Who was he kidding? She wasn't leaving Montana, she was leaving *him*. If she cared about him even a little, she would give him some signal that she wanted to stay, or at least find a way to be together despite the distance. Instead, she was probably already mentally packing her belongings to head back to the windy city. She would return to her world full of people and friends who cared about her and he would be left here, alone except for his brothers. He tried to content himself with the thought that he would still have his brothers—his best friends. They had always been enough before. But now, having met her and knowing what he had been missing, he was afraid he would spend his life pining.

Somehow, that thought caused him to muster what small amount of pride remained. He was Cade King. He pined for no girl, not even Layla. For the duration of her stay, he would be friendly only as much as was required. He would continue to spend his days outdoors, never hinting at how much he wanted to be with her.

The nagging thought that she was the one who made it possible for him to go outside wouldn't go away. He turned on music to try and drown it out. When that didn't work, he wheeled himself to his room and went to bed, stuffing the pillow over his face in an attempt to stop his torturous thoughts.

* * *

THE NEXT TWO days were horrible. Layla and Cade tiptoed around each other, avoiding contact as much as possible. He rose early to eat breakfast with his brothers and stayed outside until they came in so he wouldn't have to be alone with Layla. He was sure she saw through his pathetic attempts to avoid her, but he was wrong.

Layla thought his absence was a way of proving to her that he had never wanted her in his life in the first place. He had his ranch and his brothers again; what did he need her for? The imagined rebuff was painful, but on some level she was happy for him. She had accomplished what she set out to do, at least in some part. Cade was beginning to get his life back. No longer confined to the house, he was free to be outside, soaking up the fresh air with his brothers. And soon he would be able to ride again, too.

That day came three days after their tiff. A delivery truck rolled up to the barn, and Layla's heart started to pound. She wished she could be there to see Cade's face when he opened the package, but he was outside. When Coy entered the house a few minutes later, he found her with her face pressed to the window, hoping for a glimpse of Cade's reaction.

"What are you doing?" he asked.

Startled, she whirled and dropped the measuring cup she forgot she was holding. "Nothing," she lied. "Just looking outside." She smiled. "I bet deliverymen hate coming out here." The ranch was well off the beaten path. It would probably take a driver all day to reach this place.

Coy nodded. "My guess is they argue over who has to do it. Today's driver looked new. He probably drew the short end of the stick." He stopped and studied her. Cade had said she was dying to get back to Chicago, but Coy wasn't so sure. The soulful look on her face as she stared out the window didn't resemble someone who was homesick. It looked more like lovesickness to him.

"Come on," he said, holding out his hand to her.

"Where?" she asked.

"To the barn. We haven't given Cade the package yet."

She backed away a step until she bumped the counter. "I'm not sure I should go. I don't think he wants me there."

What we have here is a failure to communicate, thought Coy. He was irritated with both of them. Why couldn't they just talk to each other? They would save so much time and trouble if they laid things out and cleared the air between them. What they needed was some uninterrupted time together, and he knew just how to make that happen. He smiled wickedly, clasped her hand, and pulled her behind him. She blathered more protests, but he tuned her out.

He stopped when they reached the office. His brothers were already there. Cade looked up at Layla with a combination of hope and resentment before quickly wiping his expression clean. He turned dull eyes back to the package in front of him. They hadn't told him anything about it, so he showed no signs of curiosity, only an impatience to get whatever this was over with so he could go back to avoiding Layla.

Not today, Coy thought. *You two are going to spend time together if I have to tie you together.*

Cam opened the package without ceremony. Josh helped him pull the saddle away from its packaging.

"What's that?" Cade asked, intrigued. Obviously it was a saddle, but not like any he had ever seen. Were they testing a new product?

"It's your saddle," Cam announced. His toneless voice alerted Cade to the fact that he was suppressing some emotion. Of all of them, Cam was the worst at dealing with his feelings. Whenever a pesky emotion arose, he tamped it down and cut it off, becoming almost robotic.

"Is this some sort of joke?" Cade asked. "What am I supposed to use that for, decoration?"

Cam shook his head. "It's a special saddle. Layla did some research."

She wished he would have kept her out of it. All eyes swiveled to her, waiting for her to explain the saddle. "It's specially designed for people who can't use their legs," she said with uncharacteristic shyness. So far, he wasn't reacting well to the sight of the saddle. She didn't want him to use his resentment of her as an excuse to keep him away from it.

But she needn't have worried. His eyes fastened hungrily on the saddle. He reached out a tentative hand to touch it. "I can ride again?"

"Uh huh," Cam said, dropping it on the table. "I'll leave it to you to figure out how." He disappeared, almost into thin air. Nothing could clear a room of cowboys faster than a tender moment. Josh followed Cam, leaving only Coy and Layla behind.

"Let's try it on for size," Coy said.

Cade looked up in suspicion at his brother's cheerful tone. He was up to something. Coy grabbed the saddle, hefted it over his shoulder, and walked to the stable. Cade watched as he pulled his horse from the stall, biting his lip to swallow down his almost overwhelming emotion. He hadn't let himself dream he would ride his horse again. Seeing his mare had been too painful, so he had stayed away. Now she came out of her stall with her ears pricked toward him, whinnying happily at the sight of him. Apparently she had missed him as much as he missed her, and he suddenly felt bad about staying away for so long.

"Hi, girl," he said. She pranced happily while Coy expertly attached the new saddle. They held their breath to see if the horse would react badly to the new arrangement. But they should have known better. She was sweet-natured and easygoing. After a curious glance at the new saddle, she stood patiently, waiting for Cade to ascend.

"Now what?" Cade said, trying to imagine how he would get from his chair into the saddle.

Coy stood back and stared at the horse, too. It was one thing to lift his brother a few inches from his chair to a bed, but lifting him over his head and onto a horse might be more than he could handle. Despite his weight loss, he was still heavy. Then inspiration struck. Without a word, he sped off, returning a few minutes later with the hydraulic lift. Cade grinned at him, rolled himself onto the lift, and used the controls to push himself up to the horse's height.

Coy held the horse's reins in case she was frightened of the lift, but she remained patient and calm, an indication of her excellent breeding and training. Cade sweated a little as he maneuvered himself from the lift to the saddle. The height wasn't even, and there was space between the lift and the horse, causing a breathless moment where he had to drop a few inches into the saddle.

But then it was done. He buckled his legs into the strange fastenings, noting the differences between this saddle and the one he had previously used. Right away, he noticed his center of gravity had changed. Instead of gripping the horse with his legs, he now had to find stability with his abdomen. With any other horse, he would have been leery to take the reins and start to walk, but he and his horse were attuned to each other. She would heed his verbal commands until he learned how to control her with his body.

"Wait," Coy said, stopping him in his tracks. "Layla's going to go with you."

Layla and Cade stared at him in horror. Didn't he know they were avoiding each other? Of course he did, they both thought. He was scheming.

"I don't think," Layla began.

"She doesn't…" Cade started, but Coy spoke, talking loudly over both of them.

"The saddle was her idea." That shut Cade up. "And you shouldn't go out alone on your first time in the saddle." The thought of Cade being unsafe shut Layla up. Now she wanted to go to make sure he would be all right. At the time she didn't consider the fact that she had never been on a horse, and if something should happen she would have no way of figuring out how to get help.

Coy chose their gentlest mount, saddled her, and lifted Layla up. Nervously, she gripped the pommel and stared at the horse's dappled head. "Are you sure about this?"

"This old girl is so old she's practically glue. You'll be fine."

"Glue," Layla repeated. "What does that mean?"

Cade sputtered a laugh at her appalled expression.

"Uh," Coy looked caught. He didn't want to have to tell this city girl the realities of animal life. "Cade will explain. You two have fun. Don't hurry back." With one final wave, he turned and walked back to the office.

"What did he mean about glue?" Layla asked.

"When horses outlive their usefulness, they're sometimes made into glue. Or dog food."

She blinked at him in astonishment and gave a forlorn look to the horse.

"We don't do that," Cade hastened to add. "We let them live out their lives for as long as we can, and then we bury them on the ranch."

"Oh." She sat back, relieved. "How do I make this thing go?"

"Touch your heels gently to her sides and cluck your tongue." As for him, he clucked his tongue and told his horse to "Giddup." For a second, she hesitated, confused by the lack of pressure on her flank, but then she fell in line and began walking.

They walked in silence. Cade was attuning himself to his new saddle, trying to acquaint himself with his new center of gravity, and secretly wondering how long it would be before he was able to run his horse. Layla did some adjusting of her own. After a few minutes of holding herself stiffly in the saddle, she relaxed and began to enjoy the scenery. It was breathtaking.

In the distance, a couple of mountains dotted the landscape, their tops frosted even in early June. They crossed a small stream, the horses picking their way delicately across the rocks. The bare yard, worn down by generations of traffic, gave way to meadows dotted with every color wildflower.

"It's spectacular," she whispered.

Cade glanced at her, jogged out of his own thoughts. The expression on her face was awed as she took in the landscape, but he frowned. If she liked it here so much, why was she so anxious to rush back to Chicago? Her eyes widened when a large bird soared in the distance.

"An eagle," he said.

"A bald eagle?" she said, sitting forward excitedly.

He shook his head. "A golden, although some times we get some balds as well." Her enthusiastic response compelled him to keep going. He pointed out things he knew she would enjoy, such as their ancient family cemetery. No one had been buried there for a couple of generations, but they still kept it up and maintained the graves, and every Memorial Day they set out flowers in remembrance.

"There is my ancestor's original homestead. My family was some of the first white settlers here, even before it became a territory." A quick glance showed her completely absorbed by his narrative. "You never took that tour with Josh, did you?"

She shook her head.

"Why not?"

She gripped the pommel and stared fixedly at the horizon. "Because I didn't want to go with anyone but you."

They both frowned over that statement, she because she hadn't meant to reveal so much of herself, and he because he didn't understand her. How could she be so anxious to get away, and yet at the same time seem to care so much about everything here?

He stopped talking then and they rode in awkward silence for awhile. After another mile, the copious amounts of coffee he'd consumed that morning began to catch up with him. He shifted uncomfortably in the saddle.

"Do you mind if we go back now?" Layla asked.

He looked at her in surprise, wondering why she now sounded like she would rather be anyplace than there. Had he misread her interest in the ranch? "Is everything all right?"

She nodded, her cheeks flushing a soft shade of pink. "It's just that I drank a lot of coffee this morning, and, well, I don't think I can get down off the horse by myself."

He smiled and laughed. "Same here," he said. She giggled, then broke off with a groan.

"Let's hurry," she said.

He showed her how to speed up her horse and signaled to his to do the same. They made record time getting back to the house, but there was no one around.

"Not good," he said nervously.

She bit back a giggle. "Don't make me laugh."

"I'm not trying to," he said, his urgency growing.

She giggled again at his pinched expression. "I mean it, you have to stop making me laugh or there's going to be an emergency situation here."

"Here, too," he said. "And since you're the one who has to do the laundry, you'd better figure out how to get us down from here."

She bent over, laughing and groaning at the same time. "Cade," she said between her laughter. "Stop being funny."

He threw her a smile over his shoulder because he had hit on the perfect plan. "Follow me," he said. Ducking their heads, he led the horses straight into the office where Coy and Cam were on the phone and computer, respectively.

"Layla and I are done with our ride now and would like to get down," he said. His subdued tone was a stark contrast to Layla's pain-filled laughter and the other brothers' quiet surprise.

"Okay," Coy drawled, still too stunned to move.

"*Now*," Cade reiterated. His urgent tone caused them to spring into action. Soon, Layla was off her horse and sprinting for her bathroom. She didn't look back to see how Cade fared, but since he was wearing the same pants to supper that night, she figured he must have made it okay.

CHAPTER 17

That night at supper, Layla began to hope again that all wasn't lost with Cade. Occasionally, he caught her eye and smiled across the table as the meal progressed. Once he even winked, causing her to blush and drop her gaze to the table. She didn't ever remember blushing so furiously before and that alone was embarrassing. She preferred to think of herself as a strong and independent woman, and not as one who easily blushes over a simple gesture from a handsome man. A very handsome man, she thought. Smiling, she looked up and winked at him, causing him to stifle a laugh and drop his head. There, that was better.

They were attuned to each other, but oblivious to the other brothers who watched them with secret smiles of their own. Finally, things were getting back on track. Together the brothers had already decided that if Cade didn't get his act together where Layla was concerned, they were going to thump him, even if he was in a wheelchair now.

As supper was winding down, Layla was about to clear the table when the sound of tires crunching on gravel alerted them to a visitor. This was the first visitor they had received since Layla's arrival, and the timing was suspicious. Coy and Josh retrieved their guns while

Cam strode cautiously to the door. Cade wheeled closer to Layla and hovered protectively.

Voices spoke in the entryway. Layla heard the soft murmur of a woman's voice and relaxed, but Cade didn't. If anything, he looked more tense, and so did the other brothers as they reentered the room, a very pretty blond trailing in their wake.

"Cade, Bet is here," Cam announced. By the way he then immediately cleared out of the room, Layla guessed Bet was one of Cade's former flames. Cam wouldn't want to be around for any fireworks.

And, indeed, Bet only had eyes for Cade. "Hello, Cade," she said softly. "You're looking good."

Cade nodded. "Thanks, Bet. You, too."

"Can we talk?" she asked.

"Sure," he replied. He turned, leading the way toward the den. In their absence, Layla and Coy stared at each other over the table. Somewhere along the way, Josh had sneaked out behind Cam.

"Dishes," Layla murmured. She began clearing while Coy helped. She stacked and rinsed the dishes, trying to allay her roaring curiosity until at last she couldn't take it anymore.

"What kind of name is Bet anyway?" she burst forth.

Coy chuckled, took a plate from her, and set it in the dishwasher. "A nickname. For Elizabeth."

They worked in silence awhile longer. Unknown to Layla, she was clashing the dishes together with gathering force until at last Coy grabbed her hands to stop her.

"Woman, go stake your claim," he said, letting her go.

With only a pause to flick soapsuds at his smug, grinning face, she arranged three cups and a coffee carafe on a tray and walked sedately to the den. The voices from within were muted with intensity. She hesitated before knocking, and then plunged in.

"Come in," Cade called. Did she sense a note of relief in his voice, or was it her imagination?

"Coffee," she announced brightly. She carried the tray in, set it on the coffee table and held up a cup in Bet's direction. "Would you care for a cup?" She couldn't bring herself to say the other girl's name.

Were her parents rampant gamblers, or something? Was her brother named Poker Chip?

"Sure," Bet said warily. Her eyes weren't unfriendly until she looked down and saw three coffee cups on the tray. Layla prepared a cup for Cade exactly as he liked it and handed it to him without making eye contact. If she read any smugness in his expression, she would be tempted to drop the hot liquid in his lap, even if he couldn't feel it.

"Bet, this is Layla, she's our…" He trailed off, unable to label Layla as their housekeeper, but unwilling to divulge the true reason for her stay.

"I'm their housekeeper," Layla volunteered. She gave Bet a bright smile.

"Yes, I heard all about you in town," Bet replied.

"Bet seemed to think you and Coy were an item," Cade said. He sipped his coffee and eyed Layla over the rim of his mug.

"A common misconception," Layla said. Cade sputtered a laugh and choked on his drink.

"So you're not with Coy," Bet said. "I guess the gossip mill got it wrong when they said you met online and he brought you out here for that purpose."

Perplexed by how very off the gossip mill was, Layla stared at her in bewilderment. "No, that's not it at all," she said.

"You see, last time the brothers were in town a couple of months ago, they stopped in at the internet café, and one of them left himself logged in. Some, ah, interesting correspondence was on the screen," Bet supplied.

Layla couldn't help it; she was immediately drawn in to the gossip. "Really?" She heard the intense interest in her question and toned it down by sipping her coffee. "Whoever someone was talking to, it wasn't me. Cade can tell you I'm not one much for computers." She and Cade shared a smile over the coffee table.

"Cade hasn't told me anything about you," Bet said. She also turned to look at Cade.

"Layla has been with us a few weeks. She cooks and cleans for us, but we don't really like to think of her as an employee. She's more like a member of the family. Like our aunt, or something," Cade said. His eyes sparkled at Layla, daring her to respond as he knew she wanted to. Bet looked at her, too, trying to size up whether or not she believed the aunt comparison.

"How old are you?" Bet asked.

"Eighteen," Layla answered.

"That's very young to be a housekeeper," Bet replied. "Where are you from?"

"A career has to start sometime," Layla said, smiling while she side-stepped the issue of where she came from. "Do you work?"

Bet nodded. "I wait tables at a restaurant in town."

Interesting, Cade thought. Bet was actually a waitress at a sleazy bar, something they had argued over more than once during the course of their friendship. She always insisted the tips were good and she wasn't ashamed of what she did, but now she edited her job in front of Layla. And Layla unabashedly told Bet she was a housekeeper, although that wasn't true. He frowned as he studied the two. Women were beyond his understanding. One thing was for certain, though. Layla was jealous, and that made Cade very happy, indeed.

He leaned forward and filled Bet's cup with more coffee. "How's your family, Bet?"

"Fine." She looked and sounded baffled by the question. He didn't get along with anyone in her family, especially not her brother, Leo. The two had been enemies almost from birth.

"Leo still working at the feed mill?" he asked.

"Yes." She began to look either uncomfortable or suspicious, or both. Clearly, he wasn't the same Cade she had expected, and she had no idea what to do with the new one. She took another delicate sip of her coffee before setting the cup on the tray. "I should probably get going." She stood and turned to Layla. "It was, uh, nice to meet you, Layla."

"And the same to you." Once again, Layla found herself unable to say the other girl's name. Who called a grown woman Bet? Not her.

"Maybe I'll see you around sometime," she added. To her satisfaction, Bet looked underwhelmed by that news.

"Maybe so," Bet said glumly. She gave them a faint smile and let herself out.

Cade and Layla stared at each other in silence. There was something in his look, something she couldn't place, but didn't like, all the same.

"You're jealous," he said.

She sat up straight. "Me?"

He nodded, smiling.

She set her coffee mug on the tray with a clatter and stood. "Maybe I'm jealous, but you're cocky, and that's much worse." She tuned him out and began arranging the tray, but before she could pick it up, he grabbed her waist and pulled her into his lap.

"If I'm cocky, then it's all your fault."

"My fault?" Her voice was a little breathless, as it always was when she was this close to him.

"Your fault," he reiterated. He tightened his grip on her by crossing his arms and cinching her closer.

She responded by putting her hand on his chest to try and gain some leverage, but then her traitorous hand snaked up to twine in his hair. "How is it my fault?"

His left hand maintained a tight grasp on her while his right arm broke free. He used the hand of that arm to cup her cheek, stroking her jaw with his thumb. "Because any man would be cocky if a girl like you was jealous over him," he said, very softly. She closed her eyes and tipped her face up, and then found herself unceremoniously tossed to the floor.

She made an "oof" sound as her behind hit the floor and bounced. Before she could rally enough to become angry with Cade for pitching her away, she realized he was bent over and rubbing furiously at his shin.

"What's wrong?" she asked. "What happened?"

"Leg cramp," he bit out.

She sat up on her knees, brushing his hands aside, and then she began to massage. For a minute, he remained sitting forward, his face grimacing with pain and tension. Eventually, his expression eased until he sat back with a sigh.

"Sorry," he said. "I didn't mean to toss you like that. It was a bad one and took me by surprise." Inside, he was mentally flogging himself for ruining yet another moment with her. This time he was sure she was upset with him. She sat on the floor, her head tipped to the side as she studied him with a serious expression. Was she deciding he was too much work for her? Of course she was. What other girl had to stop in the middle of a tender moment to massage her guy's aching shin?

"How do you have leg cramps if you don't have feeling in your legs?" she asked.

The question caught him off guard. She was always thinking something different than he thought she should be, it seemed. And so far, what she was thinking was always better than he could have hoped. Maybe she didn't loathe him for ruining the moment. "I never said I didn't have feeling."

"You said you'll never walk again," she reminded him.

He nodded. "That's true. That's what they told me. There was too much damage for my nerves to recover enough to perform the complex act of walking. But not so much damage that I'm completely paralyzed. I do have sensation and some movement. It's weak and sporadic, but it's there." And sometimes, like just now, the pain was agonizing as his nerves stood to attention and fired at will.

"Hmm." She was still rubbing her hand up and down his leg. The action was too light for him to feel much, but knowing that she was touching him was enough to remind him of their earlier aborted kiss attempt. He was about to pull her up to sit in his lap when she spoke again.

"What about physical therapy? Did you ever go?"

He shook his head. "They wanted me to, but...but I didn't want to." That wasn't the whole truth, but there was no need to go into any more details tonight.

"I should probably finish up in the kitchen and get to bed," she said, distractedly. Without another word, she stood and ambled away.

His knee-jerk reaction was to feel rejected. She had finally learned one bad thing too many about him. For some reason, learning the total extent of his injuries must have been too much for her. But then, after some careful consideration, he dismissed that idea. She hadn't seemed repulsed by him. She had patiently and lovingly massaged the kink out of his leg and then continued to touch him while they talked. No, if he knew her, and by this point he was beginning to believe he did, she was distracted by something. She'd had that look before when she was thinking deeply about something.

Now that he understood she was distracted by her own thoughts, his own curiosity took over. What was she thinking about? Why didn't she share her thoughts with him? More than anything, he wanted to know and understand her. He wanted her to open up to him. But how was he supposed to accomplish that? Sometimes she was as elusive as the wind. For days they hadn't talked because of their last misunderstanding and then tonight they had appeared to be picking up right where they left off.

He stared into space as he tried to fit all the pieces together, but he couldn't. She was a mystery. He would wait until morning before he did anything else. If Layla was still avoiding him or acting standoffish, he would force her to talk to him.

CHAPTER 18

But in the morning, Layla wasn't there. At least, not at first. As soon as her head left the pillow, she fired up the computer and began doing some research. Then, loaded with information, she left the house and went in search of Cam.

Like usual, she found him in the office. His voice sounded weary when he answered her tentative tap on the door.

"You're up early this morning," she commented. Cam was always the first one up, but this morning he was especially early.

"Lots to do," he said. "Story of my life." There was no mistaking the weariness in his tone this time, but when he smiled at her, it looked genuine. "How much?"

"How much what?" she said.

"How much is your latest idea going to cost me?" he asked.

"A lot," she said, sliding her packet of information across the desk to him. He studied it, made a few "hmm" noises, and set the paper on the desk with a thump.

"It's going to take a couple of weeks to get here," he said.

She sat up excitedly. "You'll buy it?"

He smiled and nodded. "Was there ever any doubt? I can write it off as a business and medical expense. It will practically be free."

She laughed and clapped delightedly. Her first impulse was to stand and throw her arms around him. Such a display would no doubt make him intensely uncomfortable, but she did it anyway. "I think you're probably the best big brother in the world," she told him sincerely.

"Yes, well, there, there," he said, patting her back awkwardly.

She laughed and released him. A couple of tears sprang to her eyes and she brushed them away unshed. Cam looked horrorstruck at the possibility that she might cry right there in his office.

"I won't cry," she said, holding up her hand as if she were taking an oath. "I promise. But I will make an extra large breakfast this morning in celebration." She grinned, waved at him over her shoulder, and bolted back to the house.

He watched her go with a wistful expression he was glad she couldn't see. He didn't envy her, specifically. She was cute and sweet, but she wasn't his type. To his secret shame, he did envy his brother. Cade had always had a way with girls. Coy had, too, but it wasn't the same. Girls saw Coy for the lighthearted flirt he was. They had fun with him, but rarely took him seriously. In Cade, they had found that same raucous sense of humor along with a hidden depth and dark side that kept them coming back for more. Their mother used to say Cade had to beat girls away with a stick, and it was no small exaggeration. Now, even angry and confined to a chair, he had somehow found a girl and was getting serious about her while he, Cam, worked like a dog and had no one to share his life with. Well, almost no one.

He hit the tab on his computer, causing the screen to change to his private email address. There it sat in his message box, still waiting on his reply.

"Do you think we should meet?" she had asked. Until now, he lacked the courage to answer in the affirmative. But seeing the way Layla fought for whatever she thought might help Cade gave him the confidence he needed. He wanted a girl like that. He wanted a girl who would fight for him when the chips were down.

Shoving aside his paperwork so he could readjust the keyboard, he sat up straight and typed one word.

"Yes." Then, before he could lose his nerve, he hit the send button and returned to his business.

* * *

When Layla returned to the house, she was cheerful. Suspiciously so. Cade was learning that whenever she was cheerful and cooked a huge breakfast, she was up to something. And whenever she was up to something, it usually involved him somehow.

"You're chipper this morning," he commented as he watched her scurry around the kitchen, gathering ingredients.

She grinned at him, showing all her teeth in what would have been a scary smile, if not for the cute little dimple in her cheek. "Am I?"

"What did you do?" he asked.

"Do? Why did I have to do anything? Don't I wake up cheerful every morning?"

Come to think of it, she did. How was that possible? She had been angry with him, but usually she had a valid reason for her anger. Never had he seen her grumpy because she woke up on the wrong side of the bed. He wondered why that was. Most girls he had known had been moody. Layla's moods swung from happy to reserved. He frowned. Was she holding back and not showing him her true nature?

"Why do you wake up cheerful every morning?" he asked, eying her suspiciously.

She shrugged. "Because it's better than the alternative."

"What's the alternative?"

"Not waking up at all." She paused to smile at him over her shoulder.

"You're an optimist." His tone was accusing.

"Why do you make that sound like a bad thing?" she said.

"Because optimism doesn't always work out. Bad things happen."

"Of course they do." She set down the mixing bowl and turned to look at him. "Being an optimist doesn't mean you think bad things never happen. If that were the case, you would live your life in constant disillusionment. In my experience, most of life is bad.

Terrible things happen for no apparent reason. That can't be helped. The only thing we can control is our reaction to our circumstances. Long ago, I learned to accept things as they are and move on." She resumed her task of cracking eggs while he tried to process what she had said.

It had never occurred to him to accept his new situation and move on. Most of his depression lately was caused by his sense of futility and accompanying anger. He wanted to change things. He wanted to get out of this chair. He wanted to walk again. Who wouldn't? Didn't accepting facts signal throwing in the towel? He had never been a quitter, why should he start now?

But on the other hand, hanging on to what might have been wasn't getting him anywhere. It would be easier to discount Layla's philosophy as mindless idealism if his life hadn't changed so drastically since her arrival. He had learned to smile and then to laugh again. He was becoming hopeful about his future. He had left the house and ridden his horse again. Maybe none of those things was the same as before. Maybe he didn't have the cocky assurance that he could get a girl whenever he wanted one, but he only wanted one now, and he was pretty sure he had her. And maybe he couldn't run his horse until they were both slick with sweat, the way he once had, but at least he was riding again. Maybe he couldn't help his brothers in the yard and work until he was physically exhausted, but he could be there to talk to them and provide moral support. His life wasn't over. It was different, but it was still there. And still good, he had to admit. Who else lived in the most beautiful place on earth with his best friends and girl? Some people were alone. He had been many things in his life, but alone had never been one of them.

Layla paused in her work, considering him. "Why are you smiling at me like that?"

"I'm trying to determine if you're a magical creature. How else would you be able to change me so completely without even trying?"

She gave him a saucy grin and put a hand to her hip. "Who says I'm not trying, Cade King?"

He laughed and reached for her, drawing her close enough to

touch. He rested his hands on her waist and pressed the top of his head to her stomach, inhaling her perfume. He couldn't lose her. Not now, not ever. But how to convince her to stay?

"What did that girl want?"

He looked up at her, surprised at the edge in her tone. What girl was she talking about? Oh, Bet. He couldn't stop his smile. She was jealous of Bet. He had completely forgotten last night.

"What do you think?" he asked, hoping to gain some insight into her thought process. Why was she jealous, exactly?

"Was she the girl you were with at the time of you're accident?"

He nodded.

"Did she want to get back together?" She bit her lip and tightened her grip on his shoulders.

Instinctively, he knew he shouldn't laugh at her. She was apparently feeling vulnerable right now. But it took all of his resolve to hold his gleeful laughter in check. "Nah. That ship has sailed. Bet lives and dies for gossip, and you're the biggest story in town right now. She wanted an inside scoop on you."

"Me?" She stood straighter in surprise. "Why would anyone care about me?"

"Because you're new and pretty and living with four single guys."

She flushed slightly. Was it because he had called her pretty? Hadn't he said that to her before? How could he have overlooked it when it was such an important fact? He made a mental note to tell her again.

"What did you tell her about me?"

"Nothing more than what I said when you were there. I think she drew her own conclusions, though." If he knew Bet, and he did, it would now be all over town that Layla and Cade were a couple. He had never been a fan of mindless gossip, but in this instance he didn't mind so much. What could it hurt if people were talking about him and Layla?

* * *

Jason Wright was the one. Max always enjoyed it when his instincts paid off. He had known it was either Wright or the female agent whose last name he still didn't know. The information identifying Wright as the correct agent had cost Max an engagement ring, but he didn't mind. He had been engaged a few times before. In fact, he had used the same ring. He wondered if his new fiancée would continue to feel the same amount of elation if she realized her ring had been pried off three dead fingers before it landed on hers.

He debated the merits of killing his new fiancée now, and decided to wait. No one from her office had seen them together, but surely she had told her coworkers about her new fiancé. If she suddenly turned up dead, there might be questions. Of course he would be long gone, leaving no trail. But still, better to wait until his objective was complete before tying up any loose ends. He would simply have to endure her awhile longer.

To be fair, as fiancées went, she wasn't so bad. Yes, she had been excited when he popped the question, but she wasn't over the top in her adulation as the last woman had been. That woman had been so annoying it had been a pleasure to get rid of her. In some ways, he would almost miss this one when he eventually did away with her. She was an unassuming, uncomplaining sort. The type of person with whom silence could be comfortable. That was a rare quality, especially in a woman.

Still, he had no temptation to keep her. She might not make many demands of him, but one thing she insisted upon was total honesty. As far as she was concerned, he gave it to her, at least when it came to other women. He was too involved with his task to cheat on her, so currently she was the only woman in his life. But the life he presented to her bore no resemblance to reality, and eventually that would become a complication. If she ever found out the truth about him, she would no doubt run to one of the agents she worked with and blab everything. Some people were so unreasonable when it came to the truth.

Not that he loved her. He wasn't sure it was within him to love anyone. But he did enjoy the way she looked after him, and that disturbed him. After so many years of taking care of himself, it was nice to have someone to cook for him, do his laundry, and make sure he ate properly. No matter how old he was, there would probably always be a little part of him that yearned for what he had missed out on all his life—a home and a family.

That thought brought him full circle. Once he found the girl who had witnessed Mather's murder, he would be done with this situation and could move on. Maybe he would find a woman and settle down somewhere. Not that he wanted kids, he was pretty certain he didn't. But maybe it was time he gave up his life of crime and became a respectable member of society for once.

He studied himself in the mirror and shook his head, smiling at his reflection. Respectable citizen, indeed. Some pipe dreams were too far-fetched to bear thinking about.

He whistled as he tied his tie, then he left his house in search of Marshal Jason Wright. Any day now, he would find the location of the girl. Once that task was taken care of, he would move on to his next big heist. Whatever it was, he would make it as illegal as possible, to prove to himself that he didn't need respectability or stability, or any other "-ility" his mostly dead conscience could come up with.

CHAPTER 19

He was everywhere. All the time.

Ever since Layla and Cade made up after their brief tiff, Josh had elected himself as their chaperone. No one knew why he suddenly felt the need to be with them every available moment, but he did. At night when they sat in the den, he was there. He sat placidly on the couch, reading a book. He didn't say a word, didn't glance their way or offer input on their conversation, but his presence was still the equivalent of a giant, wet blanket.

During the day, Layla worked in the house and Cade stayed outside. But occasionally he tried sneaking into the house to see her, and Josh always showed up. Cade's patience was at an end. How was he supposed to find an opportunity to kiss Layla when his little brother wouldn't give them a moment's peace? And for that matter, *why* wouldn't he leave them alone?

Cam was oblivious to the situation, so he was no help. Coy found it hilarious and that was definitely not helpful. In fact, Cade was suspicious that Coy was somehow involved in Josh's bad timing. How else would he know when Cade was about to kiss Layla if he didn't have someone spying for him?

Cade was sitting in front of his horse's stall, brooding, when Layla found him.

"Are you going to go for a ride?" she asked.

He shook his head. He enjoyed the freedom his new saddle gave him, but that freedom came with a price: his pride. He had to be helped in an out of the saddle, at least until he figured out a way to do it himself. And right now there was no one around. At that thought, he sat up and smiled at Layla.

"What's that smile for?" she asked.

"The guys are in the north pasture fixing fences," he said. She continued to stare at him, unblinking. "There's no one around," he added.

"Good, because I want to talk to you."

He frowned at her businesslike tone. "What about?" Unless the answer was "kissing," he had no real interest in finding out.

"Cam."

His frown deepened to a scowl. "Cam? What about him?"

"He's exhausted and overwhelmed."

"I know," he replied tersely. It was partly his fault Cam was overworked. He had to take on more responsibility now that Cade was unable to pull his weight.

"Remember yesterday when you said math was your best subject in school?" she asked.

A part of him was gratified she paid such close attention to small, detailed things like that about him. She had also learned all of his food preferences and routinely made his favorites. "Yes, so?"

"So every time I see Cam, he's swamped with paperwork in the office. Think how much it would help him if you took over the business end of things. You could do payroll and accounting, freeing him up to do other stuff."

He tried to tell himself she meant no harm with her suggestion, it was merely that she didn't fully understand the situation. But that still didn't stop him from snapping at her. "I don't want to be stuck behind a desk for the rest of my life. I want to be out there." He stabbed his finger in the direction of the pasture.

Ever patient with him, she didn't react to his anger. "I know you do, Cade, but think of Cam. He needs you."

For some reason, that statement notched his anger up even more until he was practically boiling with rage. Cam was strong and capable. He didn't need anyone, least of all his crippled little brother. Was this Layla's way of trying to justify his existence? If so, she was bound to be sorely disappointed. He was a worthless waste of space, and that was all he would ever be.

"I don't need you to order my life for me. You are a stranger here. You have no right sticking your nose in where it doesn't…" He didn't get to finish because she turned and stormed toward the house.

Immediately, he was sorry. Maybe she sometimes overstepped her bounds, but she did it with the best intentions. Whatever Layla's purpose had been, she had meant it for his good, and probably Cam's, too. The topic of work was a sensitive one for him, but he had no call to bite her head off. If he couldn't have a rational discussion with her who knew him so well, who could he talk to?

"Layla, wait," he called. He wheeled after her at a furious pace which proved unnecessary because she hadn't gone back to the house. She had stopped at the pig pen to watch the little piglets chase each other around their enclosure. How she could be so close to them was beyond him. The stench wasn't pleasant, which was why it was the farthest pen from the house. He wheeled to a stop a few feet away. Apparently the wily little things had recently sprung free from their enclosure and made a wallow outside their pen. He stopped on one side of it, while Layla remained on the other. He opened his mouth to apologize, but she spun on him and spoke first.

"You are not dead," she announced, hands on her hips. "Yes, your life has changed, and I'm very sorry about that. I know you would rather be out there, doing what you love best." She pointed to the far pasture for emphasis. "But you can't. It's time to move on and embrace what you can do."

His lips pressed together in a thin line, a sure sign of his mounting anger. Because he cared about her too much to unleash his temper on her again, he turned and began to wheel himself away. Unfortunately, his chair had other ideas. During the brief time he had been sitting there, his wheels sunk deep into the mud in front of the gate. When he gave an angry tug on his wheels, they remained resolute. But his body didn't. The violent tugging motion propelled him out of his chair and flat on his face in the pig wallow.

He lay facedown in mud and pig waste and knew he could never look Layla in the eye again. Since losing the use of his legs, this had been his worst nightmare—that he would fall out of his chair and make a fool of himself. Until now, she hadn't pitied him, but how could she not pity anyone lying in the mud like a...

His thoughts were interrupted by laughter, deep, side-splitting, girlish laughter. She was laughing at him? That was as bad as pity. Disbelieving what he was hearing, he rolled over and looked up at her for confirmation.

Tears streaked down her face and she was doubled over. "Sorry," she gasped between guffaws, "but it's just so *funny.*"

To his amazement, he found himself smiling. The look in her eyes wasn't pitying or mocking. It was just amused. Apparently she didn't think falling out of his chair was a huge, embarrassing thing. To her, it was apparently the equivalent of tripping over his own two feet. And somehow he began to see it that way, too. So what if he fell out of his chair? He had fallen off of his horse before. *That* had been embarrassing because he hadn't even been moving at the time.

He put his hand up to her. "Are you going to help me up, or stand there laughing all day?"

"Sorry," she said again, attempting to stifle her laughter. She put her hand in his and gave a yelp of surprise when he used it to pull her down on top of him. Now it was his turn to laugh at her furious expression.

"Cade King, you let me go this minute," she demanded.

He almost did as she commanded, then thought better of it. There was no perfect sunset or romantic music, or anything else that would signify a perfect moment, but the moment was perfect, all the same. How could it be anything else? She had taken what, to him, was a humiliating event, and turned it into a funny anecdote. The moment didn't have to be perfect because she was.

She opened her mouth, probably to demand her release again, but he preempted her.

"Layla, shut up and kiss me." The angle was awkward, they were both covered in what he hoped was mud, and they were in full view of the house and yard. But the kiss was perfect. Her lips were soft and warm and molded to his with a certain amount of timidity, as if she wasn't quite certain of what she was doing. Of course it wasn't possible she had never kissed anyone before, so he tacked her reticence up to their unusual position in the mud.

When the kiss finished, they rested their foreheads together. "I'll think about what you said, about helping in the office," he said.

"I suggested it because I think you would be good at it, and because I think eventually you would enjoy it. Not because I was trying to think of some way for you to fill your time," she said, accurately guessing what had made him so angry in the first place.

"I know," he said. He caressed her cheek with his fingers, accidentally slathering her with mud in the process. "Sometimes it takes me awhile to warm up to an idea, and my first reaction is always anger. It's how I'm wired."

"I know," she said.

"You're patient with me," he said. Most of the time she let him bluster, then dissolved his anger by pointing out a fact he had overlooked, but it couldn't be much fun for her to hear him rant all the time.

"You're getting better," she said, reading his thoughts once again. "You're much less angry now than when I first arrived."

"I wonder why that is," he said, giving her a sweet smile. Of course she was the reason for the changes in him. He would have kissed her again, but the sound of a truck in the driveway distracted them.

At the same time, his brothers rode in and unsaddled their horses. Cade and Layla remained where they were, watching. A man Cade didn't know stepped from the truck.

"That's odd," Cade said.

"What?" Layla asked. She laid her head on his chest because her neck was getting tired.

"He exited from the passenger side," Cade said.

Layla sat up excitedly. "He did?"

Cade looked up at her. "Why is that exciting news?"

"It just is. Come on." She stood and put her hand down to help him sit up. He sat up and lifted himself into the chair. Previously, he would have felt self-conscious to have her watch him maneuver himself back into his chair, but since they were both covered in mire and had just made out, he really didn't care. Plus he was curious about the truck. It was an arresting shade of blue, with metallic flecks throughout. It was a three quarter ton with a diesel engine and, before the accident, it would have been his dream truck. He was curious about the man who drove it, too. Who was he, and why was he here?

Layla helped him get his chair unstuck from the mud. It took a long time because he was distracted by watching his brothers, the man, and the truck. Coy and Josh circled the truck admiringly, but Cam and the man shook hands before bending over the hood to sign some paperwork. Was Cam buying this truck? How could he afford that?

As he and Layla approached the group, everyone came to a standstill and turned to look at them. His curiosity had driven the fact that they were covered in muck from his mind.

"What on earth have you been doing?" This came from Josh, who sounded suspicious and disapproving.

"We fell," Layla said, saving Cade the embarrassment of telling them he had fallen out of his chair. He reached over, clasped her hand, and gave it a squeeze.

"What's this?" He motioned to the truck.

"It's yours," Coy announced.

Surely he was joking. Coy was known for his practical jokes. No one was laughing though, and Layla was prancing with excitement. He looked at her. "What is this?" he asked.

"You're on the wrong side," the stranger announced. "Go to the driver's side."

Cade wheeled himself to the driver's side, self-conscious because everyone was watching him. But his insecurities faded away when he caught sight of the driver's side door. There wasn't a regular door like he expected. Instead, there was a lift. The stranger came around and demonstrated how the lift ran from the ground to the driver's seat.

"You don't have to leave your chair," the stranger said. "You can roll up, be lifted into place, and drive away. Everything is hand-controlled." He pointed to the knobs on the inside of the cab.

Cade turned to Cam. "How can we afford this?"

Cam looked relieved to have a business question to answer. Emotions were running high in the small gathering, and he was about to make his escape. "Insurance covers a part of it, and it's tax deductible as both a business expense and a health expense. Other than that, don't worry about it."

Whenever Cam said not to worry about something, that meant it cost a whole lot and he intended on doing the worrying. Cade was reminded of Layla's advice to him concerning the business. "I have something I want to talk to you about soon," he said. "About the business."

Cam nodded, looking curious. Business conversations were what he was most comfortable with.

The four men and the stranger, who turned out to be the engineer who had retooled the truck, stayed outside inspecting the new vehicle for a long time. Layla slipped inside to finish supper and get cleaned up. Cade wasn't fooled by her absence, though. He knew this was her idea, the same way the ramp and saddle ideas had been hers. Later, he would properly thank her. He distracted himself trying to figure out the best possible way.

CHAPTER 20

Over supper that night, Cade blatantly stared at Layla while she served the meal and chatted with his brothers. He had expected to feel some sort of monumental shift in their relationship after they kissed, but he didn't. There was a change, but it was a subtle deepening of whatever they had, and he liked that. He didn't want the basis of their relationship to be their makeout sessions. Physical affection had been the basis of every relationship before her. He was glad things were different. Not that he hadn't enjoyed kissing her, because he had. And not that he didn't plan to do it again soon, because he did.

But Josh had his own ideas about that.

The night had turned cool and rainy, so after supper everyone stayed inside except Cam who went to the office to work. Cade frowned as he watched him go. How had he missed the fact that Cam was overwhelmed with paperwork? Even though he had at first balked at the idea of being a desk jockey, the more he thought about it, the more appealing he found the idea. Obviously he would be fulfilling a need, and he had always liked working with numbers.

Cade stayed in the kitchen while Layla cleaned up. She rinsed the dishes, handed them to him, and he stacked them in the dishwasher.

His hope had been to steal a few minutes alone with her, but it was a vain hope. Coy sat at the table and gabbed about anything and everything he could think of, namely Cade's new truck.

"Now you can go to physical therapy," Layla said as she handed him a plate.

He opened his mouth to argue with her. What was the point in physical therapy if it wouldn't help him walk again? But then he closed his mouth and studied the dish in his hand. Reaching up and bending over to load the dishwasher wasn't exactly a challenge, but he was still sore from the activity. Previously he had chalked that soreness up to his handicap, thinking that he couldn't do anything now as he had done it before. But what if he was wrong? What if physical therapy improved his range of motion so he could do more of the things he had once done? What if someday it helped him enough so that he was able to endure long stretches in the saddle? He could work with his brothers again, to some extent. At least he could watch over the herd during roundups and go after any strays. He had always been good with a lasso. Could physical therapy help him lasso again?

"The lights are on, but nobody is home," Coy said, alerting Cade to the fact that conversation had been swirling around him without his notice.

"I was thinking about physical therapy," Cade confessed. He smiled at Layla who was likewise smiling at him. "Will you go with me sometime?"

"Sure," she said cheerfully. "Maybe there are some exercises they could show me that might help you between sessions."

He blinked at her, not sure if he would be able to concentrate on anything other than the fact that she was touching him if she tried to help him exercise. "Uh, we'll see."

Behind him, Coy laughed, most likely because he guessed Cade's thoughts. Cade threw him a look over his shoulder.

"Don't you have somewhere to be?" he asked.

"No," Coy said. "But I can take a hint." He stood and sauntered out of the kitchen.

Unfortunately, Josh couldn't take a hint. He entered as Coy left, as if they had tag-teamed. The lighthearted conversation that had swirled around the kitchen with Coy came to an abrupt halt when Josh sat at the table. Josh was younger, quieter and more serious, but that wasn't why Cade and Layla didn't converse freely with him. For some reason, they always felt like he was listening to their conversations while pretending to be absorbed in something else.

They finished the dishes and retired to the den, Josh fresh on their heels. The three of them sat on the couch, Layla in the middle. Josh picked up his book and began to read, but his presence was still between them as if he was talking endlessly to distract them. Cade caught Layla's hand and entwined his fingers through hers. The arrival of his new truck had him thinking. He wanted to talk to Layla and share his thoughts, but Josh was in the way.

Finally, Layla stepped out to use the bathroom, and Cade rounded on Josh. "What are you doing?" he hissed.

"Reading my book," Josh said placidly, not looking up at his brother.

"Don't play stupid. What are you doing here?"

Josh put down his book and looked at Cade. "Bet was here." He picked the book up again.

Cade ripped it from his fingers and tossed it onto the table. "What does Bet have to do with anything?"

"If Bet was here, that means people are talking about Layla, about us." He started to lean forward to reach for the book again, but Cade pushed him back against the couch.

"Josh, if you don't stop talking in riddles, I'm going to beat it out of you. What does Bet's presence have to do with the fact that you are my shadow whenever I'm with Layla?"

Josh rolled his eyes and sighed as if the answer should be obvious. "If people are going to talk, then I want to be able to tell them honestly that nothing untoward is going on between you and Layla."

Cade thought his straight-laced little brother was probably the only sixteen year old on the planet who could say the word "untoward" in a sentence. "Who cares if people talk about us?"

"I do," Josh said vehemently. "We have a reputation in this community, and I intend to do all I can to uphold it." He crossed his arms over his chest and raised his head a notch.

"Josh, people are always going to talk about something. It's what they do. We know the truth of the situation; we know there's nothing *untoward* going on with any of us and Layla. While I theoretically appreciate your concern, you can leave us alone now."

"But," Josh began, but Cade interrupted.

"That may have sounded like a request, but it was actually a command. Go." He pointed toward the door.

Josh stood. "Fine, I'll go. But I'm keeping an eye on you." He strode to the door. "And I'm leaving the door open." He stormed out of the room and disappeared.

"What was that about?" Layla asked. She must have passed Josh in the hallway on her way back into the room.

"Josh being Josh," Cade said. At the sight of her, his heart had started to hammer. Earlier he had been happy their relationship wasn't based on kissing, but now his thoughts weren't so lofty. He crooked his finger at her. She sat and they shared a smile.

"You know, I have a truck now," he said.

"Yes, I was there when it was delivered," she said.

He picked up her hand and brought it to his lips. "I was thinking it might be nice to go on an actual date. I could show you the town." He was unaccountably nervous. There was no reason to suspect she might say no, but he wasn't sure how he could stand the rejection if she did.

"Oh, I don't know. Maybe not." She tugged nervously at the hem of her shirt and looked down.

Was she serious? Did she really not want to go on a date with him? "Oh." He sat back, deflated.

"But we could go to the store or something. And physical therapy, of course."

He frowned at the opposing wall. "Sure."

They sat in awkward silence for a few minutes, and then she said goodnight. What had that been about? The thought had never occurred to him she might reject him. If it had, he wouldn't have asked her out. Like always, his first reaction was anger.

Had she been toying with him all this time? Was she embarrassed to be seen in public with him? Was there someone else back home in Chicago?

But after his initial red haze began to clear, he started to think more rationally. Layla wasn't toying with him. She wouldn't do that. What they had together was real, if undefined. And she wasn't embarrassed to be seen with him. She seemingly paid no attention to his disability. And she had said she would go to physical therapy with him. As to the possibility of someone waiting for her in Chicago, he didn't know. He didn't like that possibility, but he didn't think there was anyone else in her life.

If none of those things were holding her back, then what was? Why had she said no? He closed his eyes and replayed the conversation in his head. He pictured Layla. What had she been doing while he was talking? Tugging at the hem of her shirt. His eyes opened, staring blankly at the opposite wall. She only fidgeted with her hands when she was dealing with some negative emotion like fear or uncertainty. What in his question had made her feel that way?

After a few minutes of puzzling over it, he sat up. Her clothes. Since her arrival, Layla had worn the same couple of outfits on alternate days. Even when Cam insisted she go to town and buy a few things, she returned with some toiletries and no clothing. Could her reticence to go out with him have to do with her wardrobe?

Somehow, he knew that was it. Just because he didn't care what she wore didn't mean she didn't. Weren't girls always worried about wearing the right thing? Maybe around the house Layla didn't care that she wore jeans and a t-shirt. But she probably wouldn't want to go on a date in the same clothes she wore every day.

If it was something as simple as clothes, that was something he could fix. He wheeled himself to the desk and began fumbling through the old fashioned rolodex the family kept in the drawer. After locating his cousin's phone number, he dialed before he could think about what he was going to say.

"I'm sure my caller ID must be broken," was how his cousin answered her phone. "Surely my cousin Cade can't be calling me. Hold on while I call Guinness. This is one for the record books."

"Ha, ha," he said. "Hey, I need your help with something."

"Okay, now things are making more sense. Obviously you would never call to talk. You must want something. It was too much to hope that you were going to say, 'Hey, Kelsey, what's up with you?'"

"Hey, Kelsey, what's up with you? I need your help with something."

Kelsey sighed. "I'm fine, thanks so much for asking. What do you need?"

"I need a dress."

There was a significant pause. "I had heard you were having a difficult time with the accident, but this turn of events is unexpected."

"You're still a laugh riot, Kelsey," he said, but he was smiling. He had forgotten how much he loved his vivacious cousin.

"So who is she?"

"She's our, uh, housekeeper," he said. Their other cousin, Jason, had been very specific in his instruction not to tell anyone Layla's situation.

"Your, uh, housekeeper, huh?" she asked, imitating his hesitant tone. "One girl out there alone with you four heathens? Sounds fishy."

"It's not like that. She's a sweetheart," he said.

"Then what's she doing with you?" she teased.

"That's a good question," he said seriously.

Kelsey's tone sobered, too. "What kind of clothes do you need?"

"Something fancy for a date."

"Define fancy. Are we talking tuxedo and cocktail dress, or what?"

Now it was his turn to pause. "You've been to Montana before, right, Kelsey?"

She laughed. "Okay, dinner and a movie in town. I get it. What size is she?"

"Perfect," he said, making the word sound like a question. He had no idea what size Layla wore.

"This is why I despise working with amateurs," she said haughtily.

She was a fashion buyer for a large, upscale store in New York City. "You're going to have to sneak a peak at her clothes so you can tell me what size she wears."

His face turned three shades of red as he imagined trying to peek inside Layla's clothes. "How am I supposed to manage that?"

"I didn't say they had to be on her at the time. Sneak into her room and look in her closet."

There was no possibility of sneaking in a wheel chair. As he puzzled over the dilemma, Coy strode past the door. Inspiration struck.

"Coy," he called. Coy poked his head in. "I need you to sneak into Layla's room and tell me what size clothes she wears."

"Okay," Coy said. He turned and left the room. That was one good thing about his brother. He never needed incentive to do something sneaky or outlandish. Cade made small talk with Kelsey until Coy returned with the information.

"Size six," Coy said. He ducked out of the room again, not waiting to see what his mission had been about.

"Six," Cade repeated.

"Hmm, that is perfect," Kelsey said. "What color hair and eyes? Tell me a little about her personality."

Cade began to talk and then abruptly broke off when he realized he had been talking for some time in reverential tones. At that point, he also realized Kelsey was laughing at him.

"Oh man, Cade, you've got it bad. Does she feel the same way?"

"I think so," he said. He was filled with wonder at the realization that he actually meant it.

"When do you want the clothes?" Kelsey asked, interrupting his thoughts.

"As soon as possible," he replied.

"Okay. I have something in mind. I'll pick it up tomorrow and overnight it to you."

"Thanks, Kelsey. I really appreciate this. Let me know how much it is, and I'll pay you back, of course."

She laughed. "Oh, you'll pay me back all right. I can't afford what you're about to buy. See you, Cade."

She hung up before he could reply, but he smiled as he wheeled himself down the hallway to his room.

CHAPTER 21

*L*ayla wasn't sure what to expect from Cade the next morning. She certainly hadn't meant to hurt his feelings when she said no to a date. But there was no way to explain to him that she couldn't possibly go on a date in the same ratty clothes she had been wearing since her arrival. Not only would he not understand, but she would be humiliated by the admission. Her only hope was that he could overcome his anger and they could get back to where they had been before.

But when he rolled into the kitchen early that next morning, he didn't seem angry at all. In fact, the way he was looking at her with that secret smile on his face made her feel like he knew something she didn't.

"Good morning," she said hesitantly.

"Good morning," he replied cheerfully. The other brothers were gathered around the table, so there wasn't much opportunity for anything more than a casual greeting. But he winked at her, causing her to smile as she finished her breakfast preparations.

As she served the four men their food, she marveled over the changes that had happened to her since her arrival. There were times in her past when certain foster families had thought of her as a servant. They had forced her to fetch and clean and do whatever else came to mind. She had done it, but not without bitter resentment. Now, however, she had no compunctions about serving the King brothers. She slid eggs and bacon onto their plates, made sure their coffee was fresh, and poured orange juice all around. And she loved every minute of it. It was amazing the difference love made.

Before, when she had been forced to serve, she had loathed every duty she had performed. Her pride had stung at being treated like an underling. But now as she looked around the table and received sweet, appreciative smiles from all the brothers, her heart felt warm and full. No task seemed menial when done willingly. A little part of her brain warned her that this would soon be over. Soon she would return to Chicago and belong to no one. There would be no one but herself to take care of. Her smile slipped and she bit her lip before shoving the thoughts away. Maybe she would never have anyone to take care of again. Maybe she would be alone forever. But for right now she was here, she had the Kings to take care of. For the time being they were hers, and she planned to enjoy every minute of it. There would be time for sad loneliness later when she was actually alone.

* * *

Two days later, Layla was distracted by the sound of a truck pulling up the long drive. It hadn't taken long for her to learn that visitors were a rare sight on the ranch. A quick glance out the window told her it was a delivery truck. The driver walked toward the ranch office, and she returned to her work, vaguely wondering what Cam had ordered.

A while later, she turned to see Cade wheeling himself into the house. She smiled, glad to see him. Now that he spent most of his days out of the house, she missed spending time with him. Still, she would never begrudge the ramp that gave him so much freedom.

"You're a little early for lunch. Are you hungry? Do you want something to drink?"

Now it was his turn to smile. He was secretly pleased by the way she fussed over him. "No, thank you. I got a package." He pointed to the box in his lap which she noticed for the first time.

"Oh, it was for you. I thought Cam must have ordered something for the office."

"Actually, it's for you," Cade said.

She had turned her back to him, and she stopped to face him in surprise. "Me?" She used her index finger to point to her chest, sure he must be joking.

"It has your name on it," he replied.

"But why would anyone send a package to me?" She had never received a package in her life.

"Open it and see," he said.

Nervously, she wiped her hands on a dish cloth before setting it on the counter. She reached for the package and paused. "You don't think it's from him, do you? The murderer?" Had he found out where she was? Could it be a bomb?

"It's not from him," Cade said. His confident tone gave her the courage she needed to reach out and take the box from his lap.

She sat and began gently tugging at the packaging. Cade laid a gentle hand on her leg. "Layla, you're not going to reuse the wrapping. It's okay to tear it."

She nodded and ripped a strip of paper from the box. The narrow top popped open. She ducked her head to peek inside, but it was too dark to see anything. Cade sighed impatiently.

"Christmas with you must be torture," he complained.

She stuck her hand in the box and felt fabric. Dumbstruck, she stared unblinkingly at Cade. He made a "hurry up" motion with his hand. She laughed at his impatience and grasped whatever it was, pulling it out of the box. But even when it was unfurled in front of her, her mind still refused to accept what she held.

"It's a dress," she said. The statement sounded oddly like a question. Why had someone sent her a dress? A quick peek at the tag revealed her exact size. Without close inspection, she could still tell the garment was perfect for her. The metallic gray color would contrast perfectly with her brown hair, light complexion, and brown eyes. The cut was perfect, too; simple, yet elegant.

She blinked at it a few times as her focus went in and out. Comprehension came slowly. "You did this." She turned to look at Cade, the dress still held out in front of her like a live grenade.

"Yes," he said. Now that the moment had arrived, he felt awkward. What had seemed like a good idea at the time wasn't playing out as he'd envisioned. Shouldn't she be smiling? Maybe she didn't like it.

"You…you bought me a dress," she whispered.

He frowned. Her expression was unreadable and when she whispered, he couldn't tell anything by her tone. "Yes." He drew out the word hesitantly.

"Oh." Her eyes filled with tears.

Oh no, he thought. He had somehow offended her. "I'm sorry," he said.

"Sorry? Sorry? How can you be sorry for this?" She shook the dress in his face a couple of times before clasping it tightly to her chest. "You bought me a dress," she repeated.

He wasn't sure what to do or say. Should he answer that question, or was it rhetorical? Was she angry, or was she sad? The answer, it turned out, was neither.

She flung the dress onto the table a split second before throwing herself into his arms and kissing him firmly on the lips. *If this is the reaction I get for buying her clothes, I'll buy her a new wardrobe,* he thought. Then he forgot to think about anything as he focused on returning her kiss.

Layla felt weepy. For the past four years, the only person who had bought her clothes had been a social worker assigned to her case. And that had been done begrudgingly when she realized the foster family Layla was living with weren't clothing her.

Since there was no good way to explain her twisted past to Cade, he couldn't begin to understand the overwhelming emotions his gift had caused. She hadn't tried to explain. She couldn't, not without blubbering like an idiot. In the end, she had contented herself with burying her head in his shoulder while she struggled to get her wayward emotions back under control. And now as she stood surveying herself in the mirror they threatened to rise to the surface again.

The dress was perfect. Somehow the unknown cousin had chosen for Layla as if she had known her all her life. Not only was the fit perfect, but the cut and color were exactly what Layla would have chosen for herself. Add to that the fact that Cade had done this for her, and it was almost more than she could bear.

Keep it together, she reminded herself, pressing her fingers under her eye sockets to try and hold the tears at bay. She had just spent a significant amount of time applying eye makeup. No need to smear it and have to start over. Usually she wore her long hair back in a clip or ponytail, but tonight she had left it down so that it skimmed her shoulders. She would have preferred to curl it, but she didn't own a curling or straightening iron. So she had contented herself with blowing it dry using a brush to add some volume and style. Maybe she wasn't the world's greatest beauty, but she thought Cade would approve.

After one final glance in the mirror, she exited her bedroom and walked slowly down the hallway. Cade sat in the living room, nervously twisting his Stetson between his fingers. Before he could catch sight of her, she paused, observing him with a smile. Living in Chicago her entire life, she had never dreamed she would fall for a guy who owned a Stetson, much less wore one every day. But out here she had learned the hats weren't merely hats. They were a symbol of this way of life, and they were expensive. The cheap knockoffs she had seen at discount stores held no comparison to the finely crafted leather and felt components that made up the real thing.

Her smile increased as she thought of how far she had come since she arrived at the ranch a little more than two months ago. Now she could tell the brothers and the other cowhands apart from a distance, simply by the subtle differences in their hats.

Cade either heard her or sensed her presence because he turned to look. And then he froze, mouth agape. Layla smoothed her hand over her thigh, straightening the dress even though it was already perfectly straight.

"Layla, you look…"

She strode forward and pressed her fingers to his lips. "Don't. Don't say anything that will make me cry. I'm barely holding it together." For emphasis, her voice quavered on the last word.

He nodded mutely and reached for her, pulling her into his lap. She sat and snuggled against him, conforming herself to the hard contours of his body and chair. He wasn't sure why she would cry over a compliment, but somehow he understood her tears weren't caused by sadness. He didn't understand that either. In his mind, when someone cried it was because he was hurt or upset. But girls were different that way. As long as she wasn't sad, he was happy to remain silent and hold her. Plus, he had to admit the few minutes of silence gave him some time to compose his emotions, too. When she first walked into the room looking like something from a dream, he had wanted to blurt out everything he felt for her and beg her to stay. He still planned to do that, but he wanted to work up to it and say it suavely at the right time.

"I think I'm okay now," she said. She tried to ease from his grasp, but he tightened his arms.

"What's your hurry?" He would never admit it to her, but he was nervous. Not about the date. Being with Layla was as easy as breathing, and he was looking forward to taking her out. But he hadn't been to town since the accident. He was nervous about being the center of attention. How would people react to him? What would they say to or about him? There was a small, cowardly part of him that didn't want to find out. In many ways, he would be content to hide out at the ranch forever.

Layla took his face in her hands and looked into his eyes. "Cade, it's going to be okay."

He smiled because, once again, she knew what he was feeling. And he smiled because he believed her. With her beside him, he could do anything, face anything. "Let's go."

She walked beside him as he wheeled himself to the truck. He clasped her hand to pull her back while he reached up to open her door. She was pleased by the remembered formality. He waited until she was safely inside before closing her door and wheeling himself to the driver's side.

He had practiced maneuvering himself in and out of the lift a few times until he could do it with ease. He had also spent some time driving around the ranch, practicing the hand controls. His first instinct was always to press his foot on a pedal, but since his limbs didn't cooperate with his instincts, his feet remained safely tucked in his chair while his hands did all the work. The hand work wasn't instinctive yet, so conversation was difficult. Until he was safely on the road, he had to consciously remind himself what he needed to do.

Layla watched him, thinking how well he was adapting to his new lifestyle. Sure, his pride had taken a beating at having to depend on other people now, but otherwise he was adjusting with grace and aplomb.

"You're staring," Cade accused without taking his eyes off the road.

"I'm proud of you," she replied.

This time he darted her a glance. "Why?"

She shrugged. "You're doing so well."

"It's not that hard once you get the hang of it."

"I don't mean with the driving. I mean everything. If I had to deal with what you've had to, I'm not sure I could to it so well."

"You think I'm doing well?"

"I think you're doing great."

She thought he was doing great? How was that possible? Then again, she hadn't been privy to all those months he had lived like a depressed prisoner, enclosed in his solitude. And the reason she hadn't witnessed that time when he barely survived was because his life changed so drastically when she entered it. She woke him up, sent him outside, gave him a purpose, his horse, and transportation. Of course he was okay now; she had made him okay.

"Layla," he said seriously.

"What?" she asked in the same, serious tone.

"You want to know the biggest problem with these hand controls?"

"What?"

"If I reach over and take your hand, we'll probably die in a fiery crash."

"But I can still do this," she said. Reaching over, she rested her hand on his knee and gave it a squeeze.

Even though he couldn't feel her hand on his leg, he knew it was there, and knowing she was touching him was enough to make his heartbeat quicken in response. He glanced at her again. "You look beautiful tonight."

"Thank you," she said, sounding uncharacteristically shy. "Thank you for my dress. I love it."

He was about to tell her it was nothing, but he refrained. It was something to her, and he didn't want to discount that by playing it down. "I'm glad you like it."

"Tell me about the cousin in New York," she requested.

He spent the remainder of their trip filling her in on Kelsey and the whirlwind of activity and laughter that always surrounded her. By the time they arrived in town, they were both laughing over some of Kelsey's more famous mishaps on the ranch.

"She really got her hand stuck in a cow?" Layla asked. She glanced in the mirror and dabbed at her eyes.

"We had to call the vet to come get it out. It's the only time I've ever seen Cam fall down from laughing so hard." He parked the truck and his laughter came to an end. This was it; no turning back.

"This is a cute town," Layla said, looking around. "It's like something from a movie."

"It probably doesn't hold a candle to Chicago. I've heard a lot of movies are filmed there." He was awkwardly trying to draw her out about her feelings for her hometown. How devoted was she to the Midwest?

"I saw them filming a movie once," she commented. "It was very exciting."

That worked well, he thought.

"Where are we eating?" she said, prompting him to open his door and get out. He was pleased when she remained seated until he came to get her.

"We're eating at the town's lone steakhouse," he told her as he took her hand to help her out.

"That sounds expensive. We don't have to go someplace fancy."

"Layla, this is our first date. It should be memorable."

"Cade, I wouldn't be able to forget this night even if we ate supper at the gas station," she assured him.

"If we ate supper at the gas station, I can guarantee you would never forget this night, most likely because we would wind up in the hospital with food poisoning. I've heard rumors about our gas station's cuisine. Besides, I haven't been on a date in a long time. Humor me."

"Okay," she agreed with a sweet smile. She fell into step beside him on the short walk to the restaurant and stood back while he opened the door for her. Then she had to lean over him and hold the door for him while he wheeled himself in.

"That didn't exactly work like I planned it," he said.

"We'll have to work out a system," she said. "I'm used to places that have push button doors."

"I don't think you'll find too many amenities for the handicapped here," he said.

"You could change that. By law, businesses have to comply with the Americans with Disabilities Act. I saw a movie about it," she explained when he gave her a questioning look.

"In theory that sounds like a good idea, but as far as I know I'm the only person around here confined to a wheelchair. The town is small and the community is poor. If I filed a complaint to get someone to comply with those standards, it would probably bankrupt their business. It's much simpler to go to the places I'm able and avoid the places I'm not."

"That's a selfless way of looking at things," she noted.

"It's a communal way of looking at things. Out here, we're remote. We depend on our neighbors as much as our families. This town is cohesive and codependent. What affects one affects us all. It's probably a lot different in Chicago."

"Hmm," she replied. "Did you know this is my first time in a steakhouse?"

"Ever?" he asked.

"Ever."

"Where do you eat in Chicago?"

It was on the tip of her tongue to tell him the last place she ate before she left Chicago was at a homeless shelter, but she stopped herself in time. "I don't go to a lot of restaurants. What's good here?"

Cade picked up on her not so subtle change of conversation. She was sitting beside him in the lobby of the restaurant, waiting to be seated. She jumped when he rested his hand on her knee.

"Tell me about Chicago, please?"

What he meant was that he wanted her to open up to him and tell him the circumstances of her life, what made her tick. But to Layla, for whom Chicago had always represented pain and fear, the name of the city brought bitter memories. She searched her brain, trying to think of something positive to say.

"The park is really pretty, and so is the lake. Sometimes I like to sit with a book, watching the sun sparkling on the lake." What else? There had to be something else she enjoyed besides the sun on Lake Michigan. "The library is nice." Seemingly, she had spent half her life hiding in one library or another, trying to escape whichever family she was assigned to.

Cade listened to her vague answers with a sinking sensation. Once again, she was blocking him out by purposely talking about things that didn't really matter. In his mind, there was only one reason for that—she didn't want him to know her, really know her. He could either take what she was willing to offer and allow it to be enough, or he could reciprocate and shut her out the same way.

She touched his hand lightly with her fingers. "Cade, are you okay?"

The touch of her hand, gentle though it was, jolted him. He loved this woman. For as long as she was with him, he would take what he could get. "Chicago sounds nice," he said at last.

Chicago was nice, for a city, but it was nothing compared to Montana. She thought of the spacious, majestic landscapes with a pang of longing that would only grow when she eventually had to leave and go back home. But she didn't have to think about that tonight. Tonight, she had only to be with Cade and enjoy the time they had left together. She smiled. Maybe the man who was hunting her would never be found and she could stay here forever.

* * *

OUTSIDE, Max Stuart watched the girl talking to the guy in the wheel-chair. *Easy pickings*, he thought to himself. After following Agent Wright's trail here, he had worried that he would hit a wall. But the rubes in this town had been only too happy to tell him everything he wanted to know and more about the strange girl in town. Apparently she was causing quite a scandal by shacking up with four young cowboys in the middle of nowhere. And then, as if fate was on his side, just as he had made up his mind to head out of town and find the ranch where she was hiding, the stupid girl came to him. She might as well have been gift-wrapped with a giant bow on her head.

But, as helpful as the yokels had been in helping him locate the girl, they were now—temporarily—keeping her alive. Even now as he watched her, he knew he was being watched by about half the town. He would have to wait for a moment of anonymity, then he would make his move and slip away. He wasn't impatient, exactly. Patience made perfect. But he was honest enough to admit he would be relieved when this was over and he could get back to the city. The fresh air was giving him a headache.

CHAPTER 22

Supper was delicious, and Layla told Cade so repeatedly. "I didn't know so much could be done with beef before I came here." Previously, she had only ever eaten ground beef and the occasional pot roast. Since arriving in Montana, she'd had steak more times than she could count, along with ribs, cubed steak, round steak, and a couple of other varieties she didn't know the names of. In fact, she had created a game for herself where she closed her eyes, stuck her hand in the freezer, and whichever piece of beef she pulled out she would learn how to cook for supper that night. The freezers were stuffed with so much beef she had only repeated the same cut of meat twice.

It was on the tip of Cade's tongue to ask her why she'd eaten so little beef in Chicago, but he stopped himself in time. He was insatiably curious about her life before him, but she had made it clear the topic was off limits. Tonight was supposed to be fun, and he didn't want to alienate her by pressing the issue.

They made it in time for the movie. Since there was only one theater in town, and since it only had two screens, it was crowded. There was one spot for wheelchairs, and someone was sitting in the seat beside it. Layla walked toward the spot with purpose. Cade watched interestedly as he wheeled behind her. Was she going to ask the person to move? He had trouble imagining her demanding that someone vacate a seat.

They reached the spot for his wheelchair. She stepped aside until he was situated, and then sat in his lap. After a few minutes, she noted his silence.

"Is this okay?" she asked uncertainly. "I could sit somewhere else if you want, but I would rather sit with you."

"This is fine," he said. "It's better than fine, it's perfect." Although, it wasn't exactly perfect because she distracted him from watching the movie, but he found he didn't mind. He would rather watch her anyway.

As the movie progressed, her blinks became longer and longer. "Do you want me to wake you if you fall asleep?" he asked.

She nodded and a few minutes later she was asleep.

"Layla," he whispered.

Her only response was to shift toward him so she was cradled in his arms instead of facing the screen. *Now what?* he thought. In order to wake her, he would have to keep talking, and people around him were already giving him dirty looks for his previous whisper. So, he gave up. Cradling Layla close, he rested his head on hers and watched the remainder of the movie without her.

She woke when the lights came up. "I can't believe I missed the ending. Again." Her gaze narrowed on him. "You were supposed to wake me."

"I'm not sure a stick of dynamite could have done that."

People shuffled by, staring at them.

"This is so embarrassing. People are staring at me," she said. He opened his mouth to apologize for making her a part of the spectacle that now surrounded him, but she continued on. "Who falls asleep during an action movie on opening night? I'm such a freak."

He laughed because she meant it. Despite the fact that he was possibly the only person in town confined to a wheelchair, she was the one who felt self conscious because she slept during a movie.

"Layla, sometimes I think maybe you're not quite right in the head. I mean that in a good way," he added.

She crossed her arms over her chest. "Obviously. Who wouldn't enjoy a compliment like that?"

He put both arms around her and kissed her cheek. "And you're pretty."

"That's a little better," she said.

"Is there anywhere you want to go before we head home?"

"Yes, actually. Could we go to Landry's grocery? We're out of chocolate chips and I want to bake some more of those cookies you like."

"As if I would say no to that," he said.

* * *

MAX STUART SAT in his rental car, stewing over the idiocy of small towns. When he saw the girl heading to a movie theater, he had been elated. A crowded, darkened theater was the perfect spot. He could take her out without a sound, then sneak out before anyone noticed a thing. He might have to take out the kid in the chair, too, but what was that to him? Nothing.

But when he approached the ticket counter, he was told it was cash only. And, to his chagrin, he hadn't a dime on him. So, once again thwarted by the backwards, barely-on-a-map town, he returned to his car to wait for the movie to end.

And when it did, he watched as the two young lovers got in their truck and drove to the store. It was while they were in the store that he hit upon his brilliant, genius plan, and then he took a moment to kick himself for not thinking of it in the first place. At some point this evening, they would have to go home. He had studied the roads around here enough to know they were completely deserted. From what the people in town said, the ranch where the girl was staying was remote. That left a long drive on a dark, lonely stretch of highway.

Easy pickings, he thought once again. Then he sat back in his car to wait.

* * *

WHEN CADE and Layla arrived at the store, she noted he didn't park in the handicapped spots. She wondered if it was because he didn't want special treatment, or because he forgot he was handicapped. She held the door for him while he wheeled himself inside the store and then headed toward the baking needs section.

Layla stood debating between the name brand chocolate chips and the generic brand, agonizing over the two dollar price difference. Cade sat watching her, thinking her frugality was cute. He had once dated a girl who, well acquainted with his family's wealth, made no secret of the fact that she had a penchant for expensive gifts. Layla, on the other hand, had to be forced to allow them to buy two dollar toothpaste from the drugstore for her. Coy told him that when he took her to town to shop he eventually gave up trying to get her to buy anything, handed the basket to an ex-girlfriend of his, and told her to pick out for Layla whatever a girl might need.

When it became clear to Cade she couldn't make the decision on her own, he reached up and plucked the name brand chocolate chips from the shelf. "I like this kind; this is the kind my mother uses." There. Now she knew they liked it and his mother had bought them, she wouldn't have to have this debate with herself the next time she came to the store.

They were almost at the checkout counter, when Mrs. Martin, an elderly woman from Cade's church, waylaid them in the aisle.

"Why, hello there, Cade," the woman shouted. Cade looked at her in confusion a moment. Had she gone deaf? Last time he talked to her before his accident, she had spoken in a normal voice. Then it occurred to him; the accident. Apparently she thought he had sustained some sort of brain damage, too, because, in addition to speaking loudly and slowly, she was over enunciating each of her words and using hand gestures to help him understand what she was saying.

"I was very sorry to hear about what happened to you with the bull." She made a motion with her hands where two of her fingers became flattened under her fist. "It's so nice to see you out and about." Now the two fingers were up and mimicked walking around. "Please tell your parents hello." She waved, as if to indicate what "hello" should look like.

Out of the corner of his eye, Cade could see several people turning to look at them, wondering why Mrs. Martin was yelling. Unable to find his voice, he simply nodded, hoping and praying she would go away. Eventually she did, but Cade remained frozen to the spot, sure everyone was till staring at the spectacle.

Then he heard a choking sound beside him. He turned to see Layla who was desperately trying to choke back laughter, her face red with the effort. She mimicked Mrs. Martin's hand gesture with the fist grinding the two fingers. "Was this supposed to be you being smashed by the bull?" she asked.

"What about the part when I got up and began miraculously walking around?" He made his fingers walk in a circle the way Mrs. Martin had done.

She exploded in laughter before quickly clapping her hands over her mouth. "Stop. She's going to know we're laughing at her."

"Come on, let's get out of here before you injure something internal trying not to laugh," he said. He wheeled ahead of her to the checkout, suppressing laughter of his own. How like Layla it was to take an embarrassing situation and give him the ability to laugh at it. And she wasn't laughing at *him*, she was laughing at the woman who had embarrassed him. What he wouldn't give for some insight into her thought processes once in awhile.

But by the time they returned to his truck, Layla had turned silent. Had he misjudged how easily she was able to overcome the incident in the store?

"What are you thinking about?" he asked, almost dreading the answer.

"Bags."

"What?" His hand paused on the ignition, he turned to stare at her.

"It's hard for you to carry things and wheel yourself at the same time. I was trying to think up a system that would keep your hands free. Maybe I could sew a bag that would fit on the back of your chair. Although I don't know how to sew. Does your mother sew?"

He started the car and pulled out of the lot. "My mother sews," he said, still not quite understanding how her mind had gotten to this place.

"It must be nice to be able to sew," she said, her tone wistful.

"I'm sure she would be happy to teach you."

"You…you want me to meet your mom?" she asked.

"Are you kidding me?" He was ecstatic over the thought that she wanted to meet more of his family. And, without a doubt, his mother would love her.

Layla flushed. "I'm sorry, I didn't mean…That was presumptuous of me. Forget I said anything."

"Layla, you make me believe that women really are from another planet. It's uncanny the way your mind works. What I meant was that…" He trailed off as the truck jerked roughly to the right. There was a tense moment as he fought the wheel, trying to keep the vehicle on the road. His first instinct was to smash the brake with his foot, but since his foot was useless and so was the pedal on the floor, he remembered to use his hands. Easing the truck into neutral, he gently squeezed the brake while easing the truck to the side of the road.

"What happened?" she asked.

"Flat tire." He thumped his fist on the steering wheel. "I think I've found a flaw in the handicapped driver plan. What are we supposed to do now?" There was no way he could heft the heavy tire out of the tall truck and then change the flat.

"Uh, Cade, hello. If you tell me what to do, I can do it."

He chafed at the idea of a woman changing a tire, especially in a truck this size. But she was right; there was no choice. "All right." He opened his door and began lowering the lift. Layla met him at the right rear tire. "Oh, man. What happened? This thing is shredded."

"You did a good job keeping us on the road," Layla said. She reached out and squeezed his shoulder.

He expelled a breath, trying to allow her gentle praise to alleviate his frustration. If he were whole, he would be able to change the tire and have them on the road in no time. Instead, little Layla was going to have to heft the huge tire all by herself while he sat back and watched helplessly. But the situation was unchangeable. He could stew over it, or he could accept the way things were and let them go. At least she was here. Without her, he would be stuck until someone came along, and on this road, no one ever came along.

"Ready to get started?" he asked with as much cheerfulness as he could muster.

She nodded. "I've always wanted to learn how to change a tire."

He grinned at her. "Of course you would regard this situation as fun"

"I'll only label it as fun if I don't get my dress dirty," she said.

He reached for the buttons of his shirt. "You can put my shirt over it, that way it'll be safe." Absently he looked down. When he looked up again, Layla was moving away from him. It took his mind a second to assimilate the odd scene because she wasn't walking away, she was being dragged away.

"No," he yelled, reaching for her and grasping air. He could only see the black outline of the man who had her and the pale glimmer of Layla's face as she looked at him terrified, beseeching. And then she was gone, leaving him alone and helpless on the side of the road.

CHAPTER 23

As soon as the arm came around her throat, cutting off her air supply, Layla knew it was the end. What she didn't understand was why he hadn't killed her immediately. Why take her with him?

Unbidden, he began to explain himself. "No need to kill your friend," he whispered. "As long as you cooperate. He's a local. People will care if he's found dead. No one will care about you."

His voice was different than she expected. It wasn't sinister or evil. His tone wasn't menacing or angry. He sounded like a normal man having a normal conversation. If she met him on the street, there would be nothing about him to alert her to the fact that he was a cold-blooded killer.

As soon as they were a safe distance away from Cade, he released his hold on her and said simply, "Run and I'll kill you before I go back and kill your boyfriend."

She nodded, too choked with panic to speak. There was no way out for her, but at least Cade would survive.

They walked about ten feet and he opened the driver's side of a car. "Crawl to the passenger side. Try anything funny, and the same deal stands."

She wanted to tell him she knew the situation was hopeless. She wanted to say she wouldn't attempt any heroics. She wanted to cry, or pray, or beg for her life, but she was too numb with shock and fear to utter a word. Instead, she sat in the seat, clasping her hands in her lap and trying to stay coherent.

He checked his rearview mirror before pulling out onto the road. "I know this isn't much consolation to you, but it won't hurt. Some people are twisted enough to want to see their victims suffer. I'm not like that." He glanced at her, his eyes narrowed. "You're lucky there. A pretty young girl like you could suffer a lot before a man decided to end things. I won't touch you that way."

Gee, you're all heart, Layla thought, but of course her tongue was still frozen.

"You won't get to live to enjoy it, but I did you a favor when I killed Mather."

When he was silent for a solid minute, she thought he was done spilling his guts. She was wrong.

"I was a foster kid like you," he said. "Moved from family to family and home to home, never fitting in. I couldn't wait to get out of that life, then I turned eighteen and was booted by the system." He shook his head. "They turn kids loose with the shirt on their backs and no way to survive, you know? I was scared out of my mind. Then Mather offered me a deal." He gave a humorless chuckle that, for the first time, revealed some of the evil that was inside him. "Worst mistake of my life, but what did I know? I was a stupid kid, an innocent victim. I didn't know I didn't have to do what he wanted. Finally, I joined the army." He paused for another smile. "Bless the army for teaching me to kill. At least then I had a skill, and I quickly learned it was more lucrative to kill for money than because someone in the Pentagon told me to.

"So, I bided my time, but I never forgot Mather or what he did to me. Finishing him off was the final goodbye to my old life. But then you saw me, and I've never left a witness alive. It's sort of sad, really. Finding out your story and understanding it's so close to mine, it feels like I'm killing myself when I was a kid. But, too bad for you, I died inside a long time ago and there's no remorse anymore. If I could ever be sorry to kill someone, I would be sorry to kill you. I know what the system can do to you. I'm living proof."

He stopped the car and pulled to the side of the road. In the distance about twenty feet off the road, Layla saw two large boulders a few feet tall. The detached, practical part of her brain understood why he chose the location. No one would detect her body behind the large rocks. When the buzzards started to collect, people would most likely believe a deer had died. "Over there," he said. "Let's move."

There was a part of her that wanted to fight him, but the rational part of her mind told her it was useless. They were in the middle of nowhere. She was outgunned and overpowered. There was no hope for escape. Her only hope was that he would be true to his word and leave Cade alone. It took everything within her, but she made herself ask the question.

"Will you really let him live?"

"Yes," he said.

"How do I know you're telling the truth?"

He looked in her eyes, which would have been more comforting if his eyes weren't flat and dead and if he weren't holding a gun to her abdomen. "One foster kid to another, I promise. I can't let you live, but I don't need to kill him. He didn't see me."

She nodded, taking some small comfort in the fact that she believed him. The comfort wasn't enough to override her panic, however, and she started to cry. Somehow she sensed it would annoy him if she sobbed and put on a grand display, so she contained her emotion to quiet little sniffles, her entire body trembling with the effort to keep herself in check.

"Stop walking," he commanded as soon as he reached his desired destination. Her eyes were too blurred by tears to take note of her surroundings, but she guessed they had reached the area behind the boulders. "It's easier if you don't look at me."

Easier for whom? Certainly not her.

"Kneel down, facing away from me."

She did as he commanded, her tears coming harder now.

"You won't feel it," he said again, softly. She heard the sound she assumed to be coming from his gun, and then felt the press of cold steel against the base of her skull. Absurdly, her mind conjured shows she had seen on television, trying to figure out what the sound might be. Was he cocking it? Was it the safety switching off? Then she realized how long she was able to run through the possibilities. Why wasn't he shooting her? He had promised to be quick and painless, but allowing her to linger like this while the tension built was torture.

He cursed and the gun was removed from her head. Was he having second thoughts? Why was he taking so long and drawing it out? Was he sick and twisted after all? Why else would he make her wait like this after he had promised not to?

She wanted to turn to look at him, but she was afraid that might be the catalyst he needed to come to his senses and shoot her.

Her eyes squeezed tightly shut and she screwed her courage up again in order to speak. "Can you just do it, please? The waiting makes it worse."

"Shut up," he bit off angrily. A scuffling sound told her he was moving his feet. Warily, she edged her head toward him so that he was outlined in her peripheral vision. He was crouched behind the boulder now, facing away from her. The gun was still in his hand, but it was pointed at the blank horizon. Asking him what he was doing would be suicide, but the temptation was strong.

"Turn around and stop looking at me," he commanded harshly, not sparing her a glance to see if his order was obeyed because he knew it would be.

She faced away from him once again, but she left her hands clasped tightly in her lap. Her mother had kept the twenty-third psalm framed in their bathroom. Bits and pieces of it came to Layla now, offering much needed comfort and strength.

There was a whizzing sound, then a squishy noise, a thud, and then silence.

The suspense was killing Layla. Screwing up her courage once more, she dared to ask another question. "What's happening?" Her voice sounded frail, as if any moment it was going to give out.

There was no answer. Turning as much as she dared, she searched for him in her peripheral vision, but he was gone. She turned farther still and saw him lying behind her, his wide eyes staring up at the sky, and a neat hole in his forehead. She fell over and scrambled away from him. Out of the darkness two men descended.

Layla screamed at the sight of them, dressed head to toe in black and wearing full protective gear like soldiers.

"Layla, it's me," one of them said. She recognized his voice as Cade's cousin, Marshal Jason Wright. "It's okay." He held out his hands, palms up in a submissive gesture to show her it was okay.

"Cade," she said. Her voice sounded strange, thick and far away.

"We picked Cade up. He's in the surveillance van behind me. He's listening to us on a microphone right now; he can hear everything we say."

She put her hands over her eyes and began to cry in earnest. "I want to go home." She wanted her big bedroom at the ranch, her comfortable bed and bathroom that smelled like vanilla candles. She wanted Cam, Coy, and Josh, and the security, stability, and comfort they provided. She wanted her kitchen where everything was arranged exactly as she liked it. She wanted her kitten so she could hold her and cry in her fur without feeling embarrassed over her tears. Most of all, she wanted Cade. She wanted him to hold her, kiss her, and tell her she was going to be all right. She wanted to know that when she had the inevitable nightmares from this night, he would be nearby, waiting to make sure she was okay.

"We'll take you now," Jason said, still in the same soothing tone that eased her fears and at the same time made her feel like she might start screaming in delayed hysteria.

In the van, Cade turned toward the window as he listened to their conversation, silent tears rolling down his face. Without a doubt, this was the worst night of his life. Not only had he not been able to protect Layla, but she had come so close to being killed that he would no doubt have nightmares for as long as he lived. And now this. She wanted to go home. He wouldn't have believed it if he hadn't heard the words for himself. At first, he had been hopeful because her first word was his name. But then she said she wanted to go home to Chicago, back to her life before him, back to her family and friends. And he knew with certainty she was lost to him forever.

* * *

THE NEXT FEW hours were a blur. Jason took Layla to the hospital to have her checked while he debriefed her. While they waited for the doctor, he explained to her how they had tracked the man to her.

"He's been using my secretary, trying to siphon information from her. She caught on to him from the beginning and started playing both sides, feeding him what we told her. I hate to say we used you as bait, Layla, but that's the truth of it. Cade's going to be furious when he finds out."

Layla wasn't so sure about that. Cade hadn't said a word to her or turned from the window when she was finally led to the surveillance van. That had hurt, and she hadn't had the opportunity to speak to him since then because he was taken home with one agent while Jason brought her here.

"We were watching you the whole time, but he was good. He remained inconspicuous until he made his move, and even then we weren't sure it was more than just a blown tire. I'm sorry we cut it so close."

How did she respond to that? She wasn't angry with him, or any of the agents; they had saved her life. "It's fine." She closed her eyes and rested her head on the bed. "What time is it?"

He glanced at his watch. "A little after midnight. I'm sorry to say we probably won't get much sleep tonight. This will take awhile and then I booked us on an early morning flight back to Chicago."

She stared at him in shock, but he didn't notice because his head was bent over the form in his lap. "But...but my things are still at the ranch."

He shook his head, not looking up from his paperwork. "I asked the agent who took Cade home to pack for you. He'll bring everything and meet us at the airport."

And just like that, it was over. Her dream of a life on an idyllic Montana ranch had come to an end with no goodbye and no trace of her left behind. It was too painful to think of the King men and what they meant to her, especially Cade. Instead, she concentrated on her kitten. She wouldn't understand why Layla went away, and she would most likely be terribly upset without her daily visit.

Jason looked up when he saw her crying. Embarrassed, she tried to swipe her tears away to no avail; they just kept coming. Jason set aside his paperwork before drawing her gently into his embrace. The solid, comforting feel of him was nice, but it was all wrong because it wasn't Cade. She missed Cade's scent, and touch, and even the way his chair bumped her whenever she got too close. Mostly, she missed Cade, and she cried harder because she was sure she would never see him again.

CHAPTER 24

Six weeks later, Marshal Jason Wright broke his foot while pursuing a suspect. Knowing he would never be able to sit still long enough to recover in the city where he lived, he removed himself to his cousins' ranch to enjoy the peace and quiet.

But when he arrived, the ranch was anything but peaceful. First of all, it was a mess. Jason had never been a neat nick, but even he was repulsed by the overflowing dirty dishes in the kitchen, along with the smell of dirty laundry that permeated the entire house. He knew if his aunt saw the house in its present condition, she would probably have a stroke before tanning the hide of each of her sons.

If their present moods were any indication, though, her sons' hides were in need of tanning. Every one of them was angry and yelling, something which Jason had never seen, not even when they were little and used to fight over toys.

As soon as his car pulled up in front of the house, he saw Cade sitting on his horse in the middle of the yard, yelling loudly. Jason had hoped to only have to hobble from the car to the house, but instead he slowly made his way over to Cade and looked up.

"Shut up," he yelled in order to be heard over his yowling cousin. "What on earth are you screaming about?"

"They put me up here and moved the lift," he roared. "I'm stuck."

Jason frowned. That didn't sound right. The brothers took care of each other, and, while they enjoyed a good joke, they had never been cruel. "Where is the lift? I'll get it."

"If I knew that, I wouldn't be stuck up here, would I?" Cade snapped.

Jason was tempted to leave him there, but he supposed if he were helplessly stuck on a horse, he would also be in a bad mood. So, he limped to the barn and located a ranch hand who obligingly helped him find the hydraulic lift. They helped Cade down and Jason followed him into the house.

"It's a pigsty in here," Jason commented.

"Not my fault," Cade said sullenly. "I wanted to hire a new house-keeper. They wouldn't do it." He jabbed his finger in the direction of the yard.

"Okay," Jason drawled. Obviously he had walked into the middle of something here. "Why didn't you keep Layla?"

"Funny," Cade said sarcastically before wheeling himself down the hall to the den and slamming the door.

Jason, exhausted from his journey along with the pain in his foot, inched his way down the hallway to the guest bedroom, and fell in a heap on the bed. He was practically asleep before his head hit the pillow, and he didn't awaken until supper that night.

When he finally emerged from his room, he wished he had stayed in bed. The atmosphere in the kitchen was arctic. The brothers sat glaring and silent, eating scrambled eggs that were brown.

"Why are the eggs brown?" was his first question.

"Because none of us can cook," Coy snapped.

"You're not even trying," Cade shot back before turning his ire on Jason. "And if you don't like the food you can go back to where you came from."

"Hey," Cam yelled, banging his fist on the table. "You shut your mouth and don't talk to your cousin that way. If you can't at least be polite, then go back in your lair and be quiet."

Jason had been to prison a few times to visit, and that was what this place reminded him of now. His cousins were all testy and on edge as if any little thing would set them off. Being a few years older than Cam and Coy, he had always considered himself something of a big brother to all of them, and now was no different. Something was very, very wrong here, and he felt it his duty to help make it right, whatever it was.

"What's going on here?" he demanded, looking around. But despite the fact that he made eye contact with each of them, no one answered. "Someone better answer me right now, or I'm taking a picture of this place and sending it to your mother."

After that, they all began yelling at once. From some of their hurled accusations, he began to understand that they weren't all mad at each other, they were all mad at Cade, and he was mad at all of them.

"Let me get this straight," he said, holding up his hand for silence. "You're mad at Cade because Layla went away, is that right?"

"Yes," Coy said.

"Then why are you mad at them?" Jason asked Cade.

"Because they think it's my fault she went away. But they don't know; she couldn't wait to get back to her fabulous life in the city."

Jason stared at him, certain he must be out of his mind. "What are you talking about? Didn't she tell you anything about herself?"

"No," Cade said. "Thank you for bringing up yet another painful reminder of how little I knew about her." He tried to roll away, presumably to go to his den and closet himself away, but Jason grabbed his chair, holding him back.

"It's time for you to learn a little of what you've been missing out on by not knowing Layla's story," he said.

There was a small part of Cade that wanted to stubbornly refuse to listen. But there was an overwhelming part of him that missed her so desperately he was anxious to hear any mention of her. "I'm listening," he said.

"Layla's father died in a car accident before she was born. When she was three, her mother found out she had melanoma. She battled it most of Layla's life and eventually became so ill that Layla became her full-time caregiver. She went to school, but before and after, she was the one who administered her mother's medicine, helped her eat, bathed her, and took her to the bathroom.

"Her mother died right before Layla's fourteenth birthday. With no remaining family, she was sent into the foster care system. When she turned eighteen, she was booted from the system. She was picking up her last check when the man she was supposed to meet with was murdered. You know what happened after that."

Cade was speechless, but Coy wasn't.

"So she doesn't have any family?" he asked.

Jason shook his head. "No family, no job, no place to live, and no friends as far as I could tell. Some of her placements were pretty rough, so it's no surprise she kept to herself and didn't make friends."

"What happened to her when you took her back?" this came from Cam.

Jason frowned, not liking to remember how close he had come to sending her off into the wide world without a thought. Thankfully, his secretary had remembered to see to Layla's care. "My secretary helped her get an apartment. It's a government subsidized place, but it's safer than some others she could have gone to."

Now all the brothers were silent, picturing their sweet and cheerful Layla living in a government slum, swallowed up by the big city.

Cade sat gripping his chair-- white knuckled. At first he was too stunned to feel anything but numb, and then the nausea set in. What had he done allowing his pride to get in the way? He had sent Layla back to the city helpless and traumatized by her ordeal here. He thought he wasn't much of a man because his legs didn't work. Now he knew the truth; it didn't take physical strength to make a man, it took emotional stamina. He had been weak, allowing his wounded feelings to stand in the way of doing what was right in taking care of Layla. When he thought of the way he had coldly rebuffed her when she came back to the surveillance van that night, he wanted to die rather than face the truth of what he had done to her.

Instead, he quickly wheeled himself down the hall to his bathroom and threw up. When he emerged, Coy was standing in the middle of his bedroom. "I booked us on a flight first thing in the morning. There's nothing sooner. I'm going to go back to the kitchen and help Cam and Josh clean things up before she gets back."

"All right. Thanks," Cade said weakly. He shuffled himself from his chair to his bed and quickly fell asleep, thankful for a respite from his torturous recrimination.

The next morning, all was as it should be again. The kitchen wasn't as clean as when Layla had left it, but it was cleaner than when Jason arrived. The smell of sausage wafted down the hall, luring him out of his room. With relief, he noted that the source was a box of premade sausage meals from the store. After last night, he wasn't anxious to eat any of the brothers' cooking again.

They were all present, eating quietly. Unlike last night, the quiet wasn't tense; it was subdued.

"We're going to need Layla's address in Chicago," Coy said as Jason sat down at the table. "We're going to get her."

He couldn't say he was surprised. He had been more surprised that they sent her away in the first place, but if a lover's quarrel had been the cause, then it was understandable. He knew from experience that sometimes communicating with a woman was like trying to read Sanskrit.

"I'll call my secretary and get it for you." He surveyed the brothers as he ate. They had apparently gotten over their animosity from before, and he was glad. He had never had a brother, instead he had an older sister. Secretly, he had always envied these four their tight bond. It had taken a woman to come between them, and with three of them still single, he hoped it never happened again.

"I have something to say before you go away," Cam said. Everyone stopped eating to look at him. "I've been talking to a woman I met over the internet."

Coy choked on his biscuit and slugged some juice to try and wash it down. "What?" he sputtered.

"We've known each other for a few months now, and I think I want to meet her in person soon. When all this business with Layla gets cleared up, I want to start looking for a time to bring her to the ranch for a meeting." He continued eating his breakfast and reading his paper as if he hadn't made the most startling proclamation any of them had ever heard from him.

"You met a woman on the internet?" Coy said. "And you didn't tell us about it?"

"I just did," Cam said without lifting his eyes from the newspaper.

"But you can't bring some stranger here. You don't know anything about her," Coy continued.

"I know everything about her," Cam said. "I think I'll probably marry her." He took a sip of his coffee and turned the page in his paper.

Coy looked around to see if his brothers were as surprised as he was, but Cade was in his own world, staring out the window and anxious to get started on their trip. Josh, who idolized Cam and thought he could do no wrong, apparently found nothing odd in his hero's pronouncement because he also remained eating placidly. Only Jason met his eyes over the table, and he was smiling.

"Change is coming," Jason said.

"Yeah," Coy said uncomfortably, not liking the thought of just how quickly change was coming.

"Are you ready?" Cade asked impatiently. After a brief goodbye to their remaining brothers and Jason, Coy carried their bags to the car, and they were off to find Layla, wherever she was.

CHAPTER 25

$\mathcal{L}$ayla was tired. She enjoyed her job, as much as one could enjoy cleaning toilets for the rich and famous of Chicago, but it was exhausting. Normally she didn't mind the exhaustion. It kept her from thinking or feeling too much of anything. But tonight, her muscles hurt, her joints ached, and her feet were so swollen she wondered how she would be able to get her shoes off.

But at least you're alive, she told herself, repressing a shudder. That had been her resounding refrain since her return to Chicago. So you fell in love and he let you go without a word, *at least you're alive.* So you live in a tiny, roach-infested slum on the wrong side of the tracks. *At least you're alive.* So your heart is broken and every morning when you wake up you realize you've been crying in your sleep again. *At least you're alive.* So far that statement had worked to hold her encroaching loneliness at bay.

Like always, she concentrated on the good things and tried to leave everything else in her past. She had her own apartment. It wasn't in the best neighborhood, but it wasn't in the worst. Just about everywhere in the city she had to be vigilant and use caution, but here an attack wasn't a certainty like some welfare housing projects in town. Her bank account was small, but having one at all was a novelty.

Though the amount was tiny, it gave her a feeling of immense satisfaction to watch it grow a nominal amount each week. And, though some people might not view it as a good thing, the company she worked for assigned her uniforms to clean in, sparing her lackluster wardrobe from further wear.

Layla smiled as she thought of her clothes. So far, that was the best part of her new life. Most of her tiny income went toward rent, food, and bus fare, but what little she had to spare after putting some into her savings was being set aside to buy some new clothes. It would take time, but she had plans to save up until she could afford to buy nice things, things that would last a long time and make her look good, things like the beautiful dress that was tucked neatly in the back of her closet.

Thinking of the dress caused tears to mist her eyes. That was why when she saw what was lying on her doorstep, she froze and cocked her head, not sure if what she was seeing was real.

A dozen red roses were on the floor, propped against her door. She swallowed hard, panic filling her mind. Had the killer somehow survived and tracked her down again? What other explanation could there be?

A sound behind her startled her, causing her to flatten herself against the wall.

"It's just me."

Somehow, the sight of the resurrected killer would have been more probable than the sight of Cade sitting sedately in her hallway. "Sorry I scared you. I wheeled myself to the end of the hall to watch for you, and you got up here faster than I was prepared for."

She remained staring at him, frozen and speechless, not even daring to blink in case he disappeared.

"Can I come in?" He pointed to the door. "The hallway is…" He let the words trail off, but she filled in the blank for him.

"Depressing," she said.

"I was going to say dark, but that works, too."

She let them, in holding the door wide so he could wheel himself through.

"Thank you for these," she said. She had stooped to pick up the flowers on her way in. "I wish I could say I have a vase that will fit, but I don't."

"They were Coy's idea," he said. "I didn't want to get roses, but they didn't have what I was looking for."

"What were you looking for?" she asked.

"Sweet pea," he said absently as he looked around the tiny enclosure she called home. It was really not much bigger than a broom closet with one room and no furniture. Her sleeping bag on the floor was the only indication that someone inhabited the place.

Cade swallowed hard and tore his glance away from the bag, not wishing to see how sparse her living conditions had been.

"Why are you here, Cade?" Layla asked gently.

"To ask you to come back with me," he said.

She stared at him, her heart breaking at the sight of his too long hair that was in need of a cut again. Obviously, he had learned the truth of her situation and felt sorry for her, maybe even somehow responsible for her. But she didn't want or need his pity. Things were rough, but she was making it on her own. "No," she said.

He slumped in defeat. "I can't say I blame you after the way I treated you." He scrubbed his hand over his face. "They're never going to let me live at the ranch again."

"What are you talking about?" She was concerned by his sad, hopeless tone. Had something happened?

"They've been mad at me since you went away, cooking horrible food on purpose, hiding my clothes while I sleep, and not cleaning or doing the laundry."

Her mouth fell. That sounded nothing like the family she had come to love. "Why would they do that?"

"To motivate me to come get you," he said.

"Why?" she asked. Certainly there were housekeepers in Montana, probably some who were much better at it than she had been.

"Why?" he echoed. "Why do you think? Because I've been a miserable excuse for a human since you went away."

"You have?" she said, wonder in her tone.

He realized then that they were doing it again. His giant, looming pride was once again trying to trip him up by waiting for her to give some indication that she had missed him as much as he had missed her. But no more. He was done playing games, and he was done trying to guess what she might be thinking without giving too much of himself away.

"Layla, I love you. How could you not know that? I want to spend the rest of my life with you. If you tell me you can't leave Chicago, then I'll come here to you. I don't care what it takes to keep us together, but I can't lose you. You are my heart, you're the reason I get up in the morning, the only thing I look forward to in my day. The fact that any of this might come as a surprise to you means I should be flogged for keeping it so well hidden."

"You really want me?" she whispered. "This isn't pity?"

"Pity?" he echoed. "Pity might cause me to make sure you have enough food and money to live. Pity wouldn't motivate me to ask you to spend your life with me. And, besides, I hate to break it to you, but I don't pity you."

She crossed her arms over her chest. "Why not?"

He smiled at the defiance in her tone. "Because anyone who can get my money-minded brother to build me a ramp and buy me a saddle and truck can do anything. I pity the people who try to stand in your way when there's something you want."

She bit her lip and looked away from him. "But on my last day there, you wouldn't look at me, you wouldn't say a word," she said. The hurt from that moment was still palpable.

"Because I failed you. I couldn't protect you. I couldn't keep that man from taking you away from me."

"No one could have," she said. "He was a cold-blooded killer. It wouldn't have mattered if the guy beside me had four legs that all functioned perfectly, nothing would have stopped him from getting to me. But, in a way, you did save my life that night. The reason he didn't shoot me on the spot was because you were there. He knew the locals would turn the earth over looking for someone who killed one of their own. No one would care if I went missing."

"Not true," Cade said. "We would care. Like it or not, you're ours now, Layla." He glanced down at his hands. "There's one more thing, something that's been bothering me since that night."

"What?"

"When Jason found you, you said you wanted to go home. I took it as a sign that you wanted to return to Chicago as soon as possible." He looked back up at her, his heart in his eyes. Had he been wrong about her feelings all along? Had she wanted to leave them?

"I was talking about the ranch," she said. "I wanted to go home to you and your brothers, and the house, and my kitten." Tears began to fall, and she did nothing to dash them away.

He opened his arms to her. "Then come home, Baby."

She stumbled to him and collapsed in his lap. He placed his hand protectively on her head, drawing her close. She cried for a long time as she finally released her pent up fear from that night. "I was so scared, Cade."

"So was I, Layla. I thought I might never see you again; and then when I thought you wanted to leave me, I *knew* I would never see you again."

"I thought you wanted me to go."

"I'm sorry," he said at last as her tears started to end. "I'm sorry for all the times I didn't tell you how I felt. I'm sorry for everything that could have been avoided if I had just swallowed my pride and made the first move."

"I'm sorry, too. I'm sorry I was so secretive about my life here. Being in foster care has always been a stigma. I didn't want you to think less of me."

"I wish I could think less of you. I think about you so much it would be nice to have the mental break."

She smiled and scrubbed at her eyes. "Now that's downright sweet."

He smiled and pushed her hair gently away from her face. "Let's go home."

"I'm not sure I can leave yet. I need to pack up my things and sell my furniture," she said dryly.

He looked over her shoulder at the lone sleeping bag. "Take it with us. Somehow, we'll find room for it." He bent to kiss her when there was a knock on the door.

"Who is it?" Cade called, knowing full well it was his brother.

"A man offered me a job as a stripping cowboy at his club," Coy said. "I want to go home to Montana now."

Layla leaned around Cade so she could yell toward the door. "You're in luck; so do I."

Cade turned to call over his shoulder. "Give us a minute. It's going to take awhile to pack up Layla's furniture."

"Fine. I'll sit in the hallway, but if I get propositioned again I'm leaving without you," Coy said.

Cade turned back to Layla. "I figure we have a good ten minutes before he knocks again. Where were we?"

"Right about here," she said, and then she kissed him.

THANK you for reading *Cowboy Down,* the first book in the Kings of Montana Series. For more books, please check out my website at www.vanessagraybartal.com